A PROACTIVE APPROACH

FAITHfully
Parenting
TEENS

JOHN R. BUCKA

St. Thomas/Holy Spirit
Lutheran Church
3980 So. Lindbergh Blvd.
St. Louis, MO 63127

CPH
SAINT LOUIS

Scripture quotations, unless otherwise indicated, are taken from the
HOLY BIBLE, NEW INTERNATIONAL VERSION®. NIV®. Copyright © 1973,
1978, 1984 by International Bible Society. Used by permission of
Zondervan Publishing House. All rights reserved.

Copyright © 2001 John R. Bucka
Published by Concordia Publishing House
3558 S. Jefferson Avenue, St. Louis, MO 63118-3968
Manufactured in the United States of America

All rights reserved. No part of this publication may be reproduced, stored in
a retrieval system, or transmitted, in any form or by any means, electronic,
mechanical, photocopying, recording, or otherwise, without the prior written
permission of Concordia Publishing House.

Library of Congress Cataloging-in-Publication Data

Bucka, John R., 1949-
    Faithfully parenting teens : a proactive approach / John R. Bucka.
        p. cm.
        ISBN 0-570-05262-9
1. Parenting—Religious aspects—Christianity. 2. Parent and teenager—
Religious aspects—Christianity. 3. Christian teenagers—Religious life.
I. Title.
    BV4529 .B837 2001
    248.8'45—dc21   2001002847

1 2 3 4 5 6 7 8 9 10   10 09 08 07 06 05 04 03 02 01

For my wife, Lynn, and my children,
Katherine,
Matthew,
Peter,
Jennifer,
Sarah,
and Kaaren.

Contents

It's All about Friends

Alcohol

The Wheels on the Car

It's All about Love

Grief and Loss

Introduction

Fasten your seat belts ... as parents of teens, you're in for the ride of a lifetime on an unpaved road with surprises at every turn.

The world we remember from our own teen years has changed, and our children face issues and circumstances we never could have imagined. They also experience situations that are universal, events that nearly everyone encounters as they make the transition from childhood to adulthood—rites of passage if you will. There is no advance preparation for parents. No matter how much knowledge of educational or developmental theory we have, it can't prepare us totally. Therefore, we may not be equipped to handle unexpected situations such as school violence and teen pregnancy, or even familiar situations like mealtime tensions and balancing school and jobs.

The purpose of this book is not to provide advice from various parenting experts. The purpose of this book is first and foremost to point us as parents to the only *perfect* Father, God the Father, who sent His Son to atone for the sins of all, who makes us His own through the waters of Baptism, who speaks to us through His Word, and who unites us with Christ through the Lord's Supper. As Christian parents, we are recreated, renewed, and strengthened through the act of worship—where God reveals Himself through Word and Sacrament—and we receive these gifts with thankfulness and praise. Throughout this book, parents are encouraged to experience the rhythm of worship—God gives to us, we receive with joy and praise—as a weekly touch point of God's forgiveness and grace, the source of our strength as parents.

A secondary philosophy of *FAITHfully Parenting Teens* is that parents often find advice, encouragement, and support from other parents who are involved in the daily routine and tasks of parenting. The hope is that parents, anchored in God's Word, will also be affirmed in the realization that others share the situations and feelings they experience.

There is no single correct answer for any situation you, as a parent, might encounter. The parental response to any situation is anchored by faith in Christ, tested against God's will as revealed through His Word, and adapted according to your needs, skills, and abilities—and to your teens' needs. This book will help you organize your thoughts, survey your teens' values, and realize that in the midst of the everyday issues of parenting, God will lead you down the road to becoming a more faithful Christian parent.

Ask for Directions

Do your friends have perfect children? Does it seem they are doing everything right as parents, and you lose your way daily? When you need directions, whom do you ask?

As Christian parents of 21st-century youth, the role we play can be lonely—but we are definitely not alone. God speaks to us in His Word, inscribing faith in our hearts and leading us to the source of all answers. And He has made us all members of the body of Christ. As members of that body, we rejoice when one of our fellow parents rejoices, and we mourn when another member-parent of the body mourns. As members of Christ's body, we are embraced by God's grace. It is by grace that we have God's forgiveness. It is in His grace that we are united with God through the power of His Word and sacraments as experienced in weekly worship and through daily renewal.

We are baptized into membership in Christ's body. As members, we have the forgiveness He earned for us on the cross. With the mark of our Baptism, and the gift of Christ's Body and Blood, we are encouraged and strengthened for our journey. We are given the strength to model forgiveness in our families. We are given the joy to celebrate the gift of Christ's presence in our midst. We are redeemed people of God who are parents of teens who have been redeemed through Christ's death and resurrection. We are redeemed people of God who pray that through the power of the Holy Spirit, we might remain faithful in our vocation as parents, and trust that God through the Holy Spirit will give us the strength to remain faithful to our calling, and faithful to our Lord.

As we travel that wild and often bumpy road of parenthood, other parents, our parents, and even our children are fellow travelers. We can use all the help we can get for the hands-on, learn-as-you-go, on-the-job training for this journey. In that regard, this book has been developed to provide the support you need to survive the teen years. For use by individuals, couples, friends with shared interests, or groups, *FAITHfully Parenting Teens* points you to God as the Driver and helps you process many of the issues you and your teens face. It encourages you to think about—and respond to—your goals, dreams, expectations, and feelings. And it offers direction for better understanding your responses to these situations and for discovering the unique joy and privileges God has provided through parenting teens.

Take Your Friends on the Ride

If you use this book in a group setting, sessions could be held in a meeting room, classroom, or private home. Group leaders should be concerned first and foremost with the needs of the group and the direction in which the group wishes to travel. That means that if the group seems to have an overwhelming need to discuss dating, love, sex, and marriage, it is logical to begin with that section of the book. If after two sessions of dealing with community and support, you seem to have exhausted that subject, then by all means, move on.

A sample session may be organized this way:

15 minutes: Check-in time. This is a time to discuss the joys and concerns, the highs and lows of group members' previous week. You might sense that a parent's highs or lows are significant enough for the group to spend more time dealing with one issue. If that is the case, say something like "Marie, I sense this issue is really troubling you today. Before we continue, I wonder if we should spend some time with this. Does anyone have difficulty extending our discussion time talking about this issue?" Then adjust the time you spend on the other parts of the session, or continue the session at the next meeting.

25 minutes: Dealing with the passage, the case study, and the questions for discussion. The group leader or volunteers may read this material aloud.

30 minutes: Dealing with the focus section. To facilitate group discussion, individuals should complete this section before the session.

5 minutes: Summary. Summarize the group discussion, then identify what the next session should cover.

A note of caution: It is a tendency in our postmodern world to place self-analysis and our own values over and above the absolute truth as revealed by God Himself. Group leaders should carefully listen for opportunities to point members of the group back to the truth of God's will as revealed in His Word, and to guide them toward regular worship and Bible study.

Regardless of how you use this book, the primary purpose of *FAITHfully Parenting Teens* is to lead you to God as the source of your strength and hope through the study of His Word, worship, and prayer. Each chapter provides thought-provoking questions to steer you toward our heavenly Father and His will for Christian parents. We are not alone; our Lord and Savior, Jesus Christ, provides for us as parents and as children—God's baptized and redeemed children.

I hope you will rediscover the joy of parenting and the privilege that God has given you as a parent. I also hope that you will appreciate your teen for the special person he or she is: a child of God who at the same time is growing, understanding, struggling, and in need of unconditional love. May God bless you and direct you in your parenting.

If one part suffers, every part suffers with it; if one part is honored, every part rejoices with it. Now you are the body of Christ, and each one of you is a part of it.
(1 Corinthians 12:26–27)

Will the Real Community...?

If any dynamic of life itself has diminished over the last 50 years, it is the sense of community. As people have become more mobile and more involved with their careers and the various activities that accompany everyday living, they have less time to really get to know one another as a community. Once people worked in the community in which they lived; now they might drive up to two hours a day going to and from their place of work. Once people lived in one neighborhood throughout their entire lives; now some statistics claim Americans move every five years. Once parents knew all of their teens' friends' parents; now mobility and busy work schedules often prevent parents from getting to know one another.

Without this community, parenting becomes an extremely lonely and dangerous enterprise. Parents' inability to speak with other parents on parenting issues can create a vacuum into which ready and willing teens step up and take control. While it may seem comforting to have someone else "helping out," teens are not emotionally or psychologically ready to have this power. They are at a time in their lives when they still need adults to set limits for them, instead of their setting limits for themselves or their parents. They need parents to back them up as they struggle through adolescence, instead of backing the parents up as the parents struggle with their adolescents. The power and responsibility vacuum has not only produced loneliness in adults, it has produced loneliness in teens as well. Is it any wonder teens, like their parents, may feel as if they are alone in the world, with no one to help them and no one to care?

There was a sense of loss of community, and perhaps a sense of loneliness, in the congregation Paul formed in Corinth. One group followed Apollos, another followed Cephas. The body of Christ, known as the worshiping community at Corinth, was divided. Paul focused on this issue in his letter to the Corinthians. He reminded them they needed one another because they were all members of Christ's body, with Christ as its head—a worshiping community which receives God's offered blessings.

We parents can gain strength and hope from Paul's words. We do not need to be divided in our attempts to parent our teens, nor do we need to be cut off from one another. For we are members of the body of Christ, and in that body—the Church—we have been called to be a worshiping community to support one another, help one another, and draw strength from one another as we receive strength from Jesus Christ our head.

I wish I had someone to talk to!

My name is Jim. I'm a single dad and the father of three children—Jan, Jeri, and John. All of them are in their teens right now, and all of them have been pretty good kids, so I'm really not complaining. But my problem is that Jan, 17 and the oldest, just asked me to let her go camping with some of her friends this weekend. I know some of her friends, but I don't know the ones she wants to go camping with. On top of that, she says some boys will be there too.

It's not that I don't trust Jan. I really do. It's that I don't trust the kind of situations Jan and her friends could find themselves in. They have no idea what could happen to them.

Maybe I'm old-fashioned, but times have sure changed. My parents never would have considered letting me go away for a weekend camping trip with my friends at that age. I wish I could talk with someone. I wish I could talk to the other parents. But whenever I call, they aren't home and don't return my calls.

I've been alone since Sherry, my wife, died three years ago. If she were here, I—we—would know what to do. But now I feel like I'm in a vacuum. I feel so powerless.

What would you do?

Pretend you write an advice column and Jim has just written you a letter outlining his concerns. How would you respond to him? Before you give Jim advice, consider the issues he raises:

> • Jim doesn't seem to know any of Jan's friends' parents. What more could he do to try to get to know their parents?
>
> • If Jim were to talk to one or more of the parents involved, what could he say? How could Jim voice his concerns?
>
> • Apparently Jim has no one to share his worries or concerns with. Is there someone besides an advice column that might help Jim deal with his concerns?
>
> • Jim says he doesn't trust the conditions in which Jan and her friends might find themselves. What are Jim's greatest fears?
>
> • Finally, knowing what you know and don't know about the situation, should Jim let Jan go on the camping trip? Why? Why not?

As we continue to grow and change, along with the growth and changes of our teens, we need help. Parenting is one of the things we do throughout our lives for which we have no advance preparation. No amount of educational or developmental theory can possibly prepare us for every situation we face as parents—especially as parents of teenagers—although we do, at times, live with the mistaken belief that we know everything.

We need not be afraid to voice our concerns to the parents of our teens' friends. Chances are our feelings, fears, and concerns are shared by other parents. Open communication will not only ease the vacuum of loneliness, it will give us the opportunity to enter into agreements with our teens' friends' parents about what is acceptable and what is not acceptable behavior, about curfews, and setting responsible and accountable limits.

It can be very tempting for us as parents of teens to believe we are alone, that no other parents experience what we do as we raise our teens. But remember that as a member of the body of Christ, we are not alone in our calling as parents. Christ, our Head, strengthens us, forgives us, and gives us hope. He brings us together into a worshiping community called to care, love, and support one another throughout the parenting process. When we are in pain, there is another parent who has experienced our pain; when we are celebrating, there is another parent who knows our joy. Even in our darkest parenting hours, we need never feel alone. With God as our Guide and within this community, in Christ, we know there is always someone to cry with, laugh with, and together, grow in our love for God and our teen sons and daughters.

Closing Prayer

O God, sometimes as a parent I feel so alone and afraid. When those times strike, remind me that You have placed me into a community known as the body of Christ. As a member of this body, help me confess my needs and reach out to my fellow members for support, at the same time giving thanks for the support You continue to give me and my family. In Jesus' name. Amen.

Parent Pairs

How often do you share your concerns about parenting with your spouse or another parent? What are the primary concerns you would like to discuss? Your teens' friends? Your teens' behavior? What information would you like to hear from other parents about your teens?

Read 1 Corinthians 12:26–27 and consider the following issues as you discuss the **Parent Pairs** section with your spouse or another parent friend.

Will the Real Community...?

(To be done with your spouse or another parent.)

1. I know all the parents of my teen's friends.

    Agree   Disagree

2. I have talked to some of my teen's friends' parents about parenting issues.

    Always   Sometimes   Never

3. When I have talked with my teen's friends' parents about parenting issues, the conversation has produced beneficial results.

    Always   Sometimes   Never

4. I have a concern I wish I could discuss with my teen's friends' parents.

    Agree   Disagree

5. If I had a concern to share with my teen's friends parents, it would be:

6. If another adult had a concern about my teen or the way I parent:
    (You may choose more than one answer.)
    ☐ I would want them to talk to me immediately.
    ☐ I would want them to talk to me only if they knew me and I knew them.
    ☐ I can take care of things by myself; there isn't any need for anyone to intervene.
    ☐ I would want them to ask me first if I wanted to listen to their concern.

7. I have someone I can talk to regularly about parenting issues.

       Agree   Disagree

8. Our schools, churches, and community encourage us to form parental networks to deal with our concerns about our teens.

       Agree   Disagree

9. The greatest benefit a parental support network can give parents is:

10. The greatest benefit a parental support network can give youth is:

11. The best advice I can give parents who want to form a parental support network is:

12. If I had a question about parenting my teen, I could go to any of the following people:

13. What makes these people so helpful?

14. If I had a question about parenting my teen, I wouldn't go to any of the following people:

15. What makes these people not so helpful?

16. The most help I received in my experience of being the parent of a teen was:

17. I believe I could help other parents parent their teens because I could give them:

18. After talking about the subject of parental support, I have decided to change the way I ask for that support.

   Agree   **Disagree**

19. In the past, I have asked for support by:

20. In the future, I will ask for support from other parents by:

21. As a member of the body of Christ, the church helps me parent by:

22. If I could receive some help from my church in parenting, that help would be:

23. The strength I draw from 1 Corinthians 12:26–27 is:

When He was at the table with them, He took bread, gave thanks, broke it and began to give it to them. Then their eyes were opened and they recognized Him. (Luke 24:30–31)

It's Always at Dinner

Set dinner times are rare for many families. Instead, most families eat between—or while—running to and from work; school; soccer, hockey, basketball, baseball, football practice; or dental and orthodontist appointments. If families don't eat on the run, individuals often eat alone in front of a television, listening to CDs, doing homework, or finishing up work from the office.

When families do finally sit down together for dinner, stress is often the result. If meals aren't served on time, or if family members are hungry and tired when they come to the table, conflict is never far from the surface. With such short tempers, the temptation to lash out at a spouse, child, or sibling can be great.

In Luke's Gospel, Cleopas and his friend were "on the run" from Jerusalem back to their home in Emmaus. Filled with tragic news—the death of their Lord—they may not have even taken the time to sit down and eat. While they were on their way, the risen Lord appeared to them. He took time to listen to them and teach them, but it was only after they invited Him into their home for a meal that He took bread, gave thanks, broke it, and began to distribute it. Immediately, they recognized Him. In the "breaking of the bread," Jesus was present and Christ revealed Himself. It was then that Cleopas and his friend were reminded that they were united with their risen Lord and Savior.

Throughout history, meals have been a source of unity, a symbol of strength and fellowship. After all, isn't that what Passover and the Lord's Supper emphasize? In the Passover meal, people join together to celebrate the blood of the Lamb and protection of God. In the Lord's Supper, Christ reveals Himself to us through His body and blood, the bread and the wine. We rejoice in the God who is present in Jesus Christ, the Lamb of God. It is our eating and drinking Christ's body and blood in communion where we receive forgiveness and celebrate our being one with God through Christ's suffering, death, and resurrection. As we go often to His Table and return to our family tables, we take with us the celebration of our unity in Christ, knowing God is present with us to strengthen, guide, and nurture our relationships with the people we love.

I hate meals!

My name is Ali. I'm 13. I hate meals! It never fails—whenever our family sits down to eat, it always seems so tense. My older sister is always on my case or putting me down for something, my younger brother gets mad at my older sister, and I get tired of both of them talking all the time. My parents always seem crabby and rarely speak to each other. When they speak to us, it's always about something we've forgotten to do.

My mother says she's tired of our fighting. My father says if we're going to be that way, he might as well not come home from work. I say I think we're getting blamed for everything that happens at our meals, and it's not all our fault. I wish there was something that could be done to help us all change. I wish there was something I could do.

I know it's normal for brothers and sisters to fight. But whenever it happens, I feel less than human, like I don't even exist. I thought families were supposed to be places where people love and support one another. My family isn't that kind of place.

What would you do?

• Pretend you are Ali's family doctor. Your job is to diagnose what is wrong at this family dinner table. What problems would you include in your diagnosis?

• At the same time, doctors heal. What steps would you suggest to this family that might help their prognosis and change their situation?

- It's one thing to diagnose a situation and make suggestions for change, it's quite another to deal with the individuals directly. How would you address Ali's concerns?
- Ali is tired of being blamed for the situation. What can Ali do to make the best of a frustrating, painful situation?
- If families are supposed to love and support one another, what specific things could Ali's family do to show their love and support for one another?
- How would you rate this family's chance for change on a scale of 1–10, with 1 being the least probable chance and 10 being the most probable chance? Be prepared to say why you rated the family the way you did.

Let's face it—meals can be stressful. We as parents might contribute to the reduction of stress, however, by considering the following suggestions:

- Schedule a consistent time for dinner, then plan accordingly. If dinnertime is a fixed entry in family members' appointment books, other events can be scheduled around it—instead of in the middle of it.
- Establish clear expectations about what happens at the dinner table. Say things like "Mealtime is the time for us to do some listening about your day! One at a time, please tell us one important thing that happened to you or that you did today!" It's also acceptable to set clear limits on behavior by saying things like, "Harry, we do not say anything at the table that would put your brother or sister down."
- Model desired behavior for your teens. They will compliment the cook if *you* begin to compliment the cook. They will also become better listeners if they see you listening effectively to what is being said. They will help clean the table if you take the lead in bringing your dishes to the sink or the dishwasher. They will begin to compliment one another if you begin to compliment them.
- Don't be afraid to lead. Sometimes, the older our teens become, the less we take the initiative to continue to lead by example, by behavior, by the words we say, and the moods we decide to set. No

matter how old our children are, they still can and need to learn from us, especially during the formative years of adolescence.

• Finally, make it a priority to feast at the Lord's Table. Remember that as Christian parents, you bring to your mealtimes the strength, forgiveness, and new life you receive as Christ comes to you in the Lord's Supper. That Meal is a foretaste of our feast to come with God. It unites us and our communing teens with God who forgives, nurtures us, supports us, and strengthens us as parents and members of God's family. As we lead, may we remember to seek God's leading and direction, trusting He will empower us to remain faithful to our calling as parents and His servants.

Closing Prayer

O God, You have given the Lord's Supper as a means of grace and a place of forgiveness—a sign of fellowship and a source of strength for your Church. May our family meals reflect the same fellowship, forgiveness, and strength You have given us through Your Son, Jesus Christ our Lord. Amen.

Parent Pairs

What are mealtimes like in your home? Are you satisfied with the number of meals you eat together as a family? What do you like about eating meals together? What would you like to change about the family meal? How does the Lord's Supper fortify the importance of your own family meals?

Read Luke 24:30–31 and consider the following questions as you discuss the **Parent Pairs** section with your spouse or another parent.

It's Always at Dinner

(To be done with your spouse or another parent.)

1. Dinner should always be served at a regular time each evening.

   Agree   Disagree

2. We should eat at least seven meals together as a family each week.

   Agree   Disagree

3. Only positive comments should be expressed by family members at the dinner table.

   Agree   Disagree

4. Dinnertime should not be a time to resolve family conflicts.

   Agree   Disagree

5. Dinnertime should be a time when anyone can express any feeling they wish.

   Agree   Disagree

6. Our dinners should begin and end with prayer.

   Agree   Disagree

7. Our dinners should take place when no one is rushed.

   Agree   Disagree

8. Our dinners should be a time when we take risks and experiment with new kinds of menus.

   Agree   Disagree

9. Clean up after dinner should be assigned to each son or daughter of the family on a consistent basis.

   Agree   Disagree

10. Dinnertime is a time to check family schedules and responsibilities for the following day.

    Agree   Disagree

11. Dinnertime should include faith discussions and family devotions.

    Agree   Disagree

12. Dinnertime should be a time when the television and stereo are turned off.

    Agree   Disagree

13. Family members should go away from the dinner table filled and refreshed, looking forward to the next time the family eats together.

    Agree   Disagree

14. Dinnertime should be a time when we enjoy one another's company.

    Agree   Disagree

15. There shouldn't be any rules for family dinners because rules get in the way of relationships.

    Agree   Disagree

16. Everyone should have an assigned place at the dinner table.

    Agree   Disagree

17. If family rules are broken and expectations not met, teens may be excused from the dinner table.

    Agree   Disagree

18. Three things I like about the way my family observes our dinnertime are:

19. Three things I dislike about the way my family observes our dinnertime are:

20. If I could change anything about the way our family observes dinnertime it would be:

21. If people saw our dinnertime together as a family I think they would say:
    - ❏ Thank God there is a family with more chaos than our family.
    - ❏ I wish our family was as silent as this family when they eat.
    - ❏ I really like the way they enjoy one another's company.
    - ❏ They must be burning a lot of calories the way they make fun of one another.
    - ❏ This is a family that is united around God.
    - ❏ I wish this family would lighten up and have some fun.
    - ❏ I don't have the slightest idea what they would say.
    - ❏ I'm not sure anyone would like to see us dine together as a family.

22. If my participation in the Lord's Supper brings God's forgiveness and love for me, warts and all, one way I could gratefully respond to His grace at our own family table would be to:

23. The strength I draw from Luke 24:30–31 is:

But you are a chosen people, a royal priest-hood, a holy nation, a people belonging to God, that you may declare the praises of Him who called you out of darkness into His wonderful light. Once you were not a people, but now you are the people of God; once you had not received mercy, but now you have received mercy. (1 Peter 2:9–10)

You've Hit the Bottom

Nothing challenges a person's identity, confidence, and competence, and threatens their self-esteem, like being the parent of a teenager. The task of parenting teens has brought many skilled, self-fulfilled, eminently successful people to their knees. In fact, we who are parents of teens may wonder at times why we ever became parents in the first place. We thought we had something to teach, learn, give. Instead, we realize the knowledge we wanted to share is hopelessly outdated; the explosion of the information age has left us in the dust. Instead of giving to our teens, we have found they have developed the highly skilled art of taking, and taking, and taking when we have nothing left from which to take.

The importance of addressing loneliness and self-esteem in the parenting process cannot be understated. Many times we fall victim to the delusion of believing we are the only ones who have problems—or problem children. We look at our friends and colleagues and believe their lives are perfect, they are surrounded by perfect children.

The apostle Peter talks about a wonderful transformation that takes place for all who believe in Jesus. Written to Christians scattered throughout Asia Minor, Peter reminds them that in the midst of their persecution, they remain God's special, elect, called people. Peter emphasizes that the grace bestowed upon his readers through the gift of God's Son, Jesus Christ, gives them a new identity as royal priests and chosen people.

In our Baptism, we also have been chosen as God's people, called to be saints and followers of Jesus. Even as parents, God declares us to be His saints, embracing us with His grace especially as we parent our teenagers. It can be very difficult to experience God's grace when all we perceive is judgment and failure, when we live in the "should have" and "if only" thinking that is easy for parents to fall into. But God's grace helps us see ourselves as God sees us through Jesus: His special, unique, chosen children—redeemed and forgiven. As we acknowledge our failures and are renewed by His word of forgiveness, God gives us the proper view of our great value to Him. His grace enables us to live Christlike lives, supportive of one another.

I thought I knew who I was!

My name is Lisa. I was married to my husband Kurt for five years before we had our only child, Melanie. That was 16 years ago. When Melanie was born, I quit my job and decided to stay home until she was in kindergarten. Then I went back to work. After all, with my only child in kindergarten, there wasn't really that much to do around the house, even if Melanie went to school only in the afternoons. Kurt's working nights made it easier for us because we didn't have to pay for day care.

Now that Melanie has turned 16, I wonder what has happened—to Melanie, to our family, to me. It seems like a day doesn't go by without an argument between Melanie and me about homework, friends, boys, the car, what she is wearing, what she does or doesn't do around the house. It could be that I'm too difficult, not direct enough, too direct, not supportive, too protective; but no matter what I do, I can't win.

I feel lonely and unappreciated. To make matters worse, Kurt just stays out of our arguments and tells me I'm always blowing things out of proportion. It's like he's always taking Melanie's side. I thought I knew who I was, but I look at the mirror each morning and see a stranger staring back at me. I thought I was a competent person, but I can't believe how incompetent I've become. I wish there was someone I could talk to, but I'd feel strange and embarrassed—like I have failed as a parent.

What Would You Do?

- Analyze the issues presented by Lisa. What do you believe is her greatest problem? What might be a way for Lisa to solve that problem?

- Lisa says she and Melanie argue about everything. She says, "No matter what I do, I can't win!" How might Lisa's forgetting about who wins change the way she views her disagreements with Melanie?

• Lisa believes she has lost an ally in Kurt. How much of Lisa's conflict with Melanie belongs to Kurt? At what point does the conflict become Kurt's conflict?

• Kurt criticizes Lisa by saying she is blowing everything out of proportion. What might be a more helpful way for Kurt to offer his opinions to Lisa? What does Lisa need from Kurt?

• Finally, what needs to happen here, for Lisa, Melanie, and Kurt to experience some peace or harmony? If you were Lisa's best friend, what would you suggest to her? If you were Kurt's best friend, what would you say to him? Finally if Melanie approached you about her mother, what advice would you give?

One major mistake we can make as parents is believing we are alone in our parenting, that God does not understand or that no one has experienced with their children what we have experienced with ours. Nothing can be further from the truth, but time and time again parents are surprised at how often other parents have walked in their shoes.

Martin Luther said, "Baptism is a once-in-a-lifetime experience that takes a lifetime to complete." As we travel that baptismal journey of faith, we do not travel by ourselves. Jesus travels with us, and God our heavenly Father understands our loneliness and helps us deal with our pain. The same is true of our parenting journey. Because we know we are God's own through Baptism, and we are forgiven by and so united with Christ in His Body and Blood, we are enabled to take the risk of opening up to someone we believe we can trust—perhaps a friend or an older person to whom we would look as a mentor. Rooted in Scripture and anchored by the Christ revealed there for us, we can begin to open up to one another, confessing our concerns, worries, anxieties, and weaknesses. With our secrets out in the open, we need not spend all our time and energy hiding from the people willing to help us. We begin to develop a group to whom we are accountable, and who in turn becomes accountable to us. Once we begin to share our concerns and tell one another what we need, we can build one another up in the Lord and rediscover the joy of being a parent. We can regain the recognition and appreciation that our teenage children are gifts given to us by God, entrusted to our care for but a short while.

The God who gives us these precious gifts is the God who helps us as we travel our journey of faith. He is the God who points us to Christ in His Word as we travel the parenting road. He is the God who remains our loving Father, who will continue to love us and guide us, and help us regain our sense of identity as His people, a chosen race, a holy nation, a royal priesthood.

Closing Prayer

Gracious God, when I was in my mother's womb, You formed me, creating me in Your image. Help me remember the teenagers I parent are Your children, a gift given to me by You. As I parent, continue to strengthen me. Bless me with Your grace so I might continue to do Your will as Your special person. In Jesus' name. Amen.

Parent Pairs

As a parent, what do you do when you feel like you have failed and your self-esteem hits rock bottom? What are your greatest joys of parenthood? What are your greatest frustrations of parenthood? How often do you and your teens come into God's presence and see Him revealed through His Word and the means of grace?

Read 1 Peter 2:9–10 and consider the following questions as you discuss the **Parent Pairs** section with your spouse or another parent.

You've Hit the Bottom

(To be done with your spouse or another parent.)

1. My three greatest joys of being the parent of a teenager are: *(Do this at home or during the group session.)*

2. My three greatest frustrations of being the parent of a teenager are: *(Do this at home or during the group session.)*

3. If in the future my teen comes to me for advice about parenting his or her own teenagers, I would say:

4. As I parent my teen, the three things I need from my spouse are:

5. As I parent my teen, the three things I need from my work or community are:

6. As I parent my teen, the three things I need from my church or the church's professional staff are:

7. As I parent my teen, the three things I need from him or her are:

8. As the parent of a teenager, I usually am the kind of person:

   ☐ Who goes it alone.

   ☐ Who asks for support.

9. I believe asking for help as a parent:

   ☐ Is a sign of weakness.

   ☐ Just makes good sense.

10. I believe that when people ask me how I'm doing:

    ☐ They're genuinely concerned.

    ☐ They couldn't care less.

11. When I have asked people for help in the parenting process, I:

    ☐ Usually got results.

    ☐ Regretted that I ever asked.

12. If people ask me for help in parenting, I usually:

    ☐ Wonder what they really want.

    ☐ Respond immediately.

13. A time I asked for help as a parent and received more than I ever asked for was:

14. A time I asked for help as a parent and was disappointed in the response I received was:

15. I believe God can help me as I parent by:

16. The strength I draw from 1 Peter 2:9–10 is:

He who watches over you will not
slumber; indeed, He who watches over
Israel will neither slumber nor sleep.
(Psalm 121:3—4)

Latchkey Kids

Family life isn't the way it used to be. Years ago, the man would go to work, the woman would stay home. When the kids came home from school, they came home to a mom who not only provided for their nutritional needs, but also gave them a sense of structure and security. These significant adults set important boundaries and limits that helped their children feel safe and not alone.

Today, often by necessity, many parents are still at work when their children arrive at home after school. Children stay by themselves until a sibling or parent comes home. The security, the safety, the sense of having an older person assist in the setting of limits has vanished from the American scene. What are we to do for this growing number of youth who turn the latchkey to their front door and walk into an empty home?

As ancient Israelites sang the words of Psalm 121 while going to Jerusalem to worship at the temple, they believed it was God who watched over them. It was God who continually stayed awake. It was God from whom their help would come, not from anything found in the mountains or hills. As such, because they were a part of the family of God, it was God who helped them hold their families together.

We are members of God's family through the gift of His Son, Jesus Christ, our

Lord. Through Jesus' suffering and death on the cross, and in the waters of our Baptism, we have been adopted as God's sons and daughters. Fortified in this relationship through Word and Sacrament, we trust that God will help us as we struggle with our role as parents. We can believe that the God who kept watch over Israel is the same God who continues to watch over our teenagers, whether they are under the same roof as we are, or whether our work separates us for a period of time each day.

It feels so empty!

My name is Sally. I'm 13, and I have a younger brother, Matt, and a younger sister, Sarah. My problem is that I'm tired of coming home to an empty house and being the primary baby-sitter for Matt and Sarah. I mean, I want to see my friends after school. And sometimes I'm scared Matt and Sarah will get in deep trouble and I'll be blamed for it. I'm tired of the responsibility my parents place on me. It's like they take me for granted. Aren't they supposed to be in charge? Isn't that how a family is supposed to work?

I just wish we could be a normal family. I wish somebody would be here—for me, for my brother, for my sister. It all feels so empty.

What would you do?

- If you were an adult listening to Sally's concerns, what would you share with her? Evaluate Sally's situation by helping her see the things about her situation she can change and the things she cannot change.

- If Sally were from a single-parent home, how would her concerns be different?

- If you were Sally's parent, and another adult came to you concerned about the after-school day care situation for Sally, her brother, and her sister, how would you respond?

- Looking at the situation from Sally's parents' point of view, evaluate what her parents could possibly change about their situation and what they probably cannot change.

- Short of one of the parents quitting work, what solutions would you suggest to Sally and her parents that would address her concerns?

- Do you think Sally's definition of parental roles is accurate? What about her use of the term "normal" family?

Economic necessity forces many teenagers to fend for themselves from the time school is out until their parents return home from work. Despite the necessity of having to work outside the home and placing our teens in situations such as the one described above, there are specific things we can do to help make the lives of our teens more secure.

Consider these possibilities:

- Give your teens a way to reach you in case of an emergency or if they face a problem they think is too great for them to handle by themselves. Leave a number that will be answered either by you or someone at your work who knows your situation. Consider giving your child a pager or cell phone so you can check in with them at your convenience.

- Give your teens the name and number of one or more significant adults you and your teens know and trust if you cannot be reached and they need to speak to someone right away.

- Leave detailed instructions and tasks for your teens to accomplish before you arrive home. Time with nothing to do creates boredom. Bored children are vulnerable to accidents and the potential of stretching boundaries beyond the limits you desire.

- Establish a predictable check-in point that you or your children use to communicate with one another.

- Insist that if your children want to vary their after-school routine in any way, they first call you for permission.

- Pray for your children each day. When you pray the Lord's Prayer and you pray the petition "deliver us from evil," pause and name your children in your heart, giving them over to God and trusting that God as their heavenly Father will continue to support, care for, and nourish them throughout the day.

- Recognize that in the waters of Baptism, your children have become adopted sons and daughters of God, children of that same heavenly Father you claim as your Lord. Bring them to worship where God will reveal Himself and they can be renewed in their living response to Him.

• Finally, trust that the God who watched over Israel, watches over your children as well and will protect them from all harm and danger.

Closing Prayer

Gracious God, as a parent, I experience so many difficulties and have so many concerns. So many of my fears seem overwhelming. Help me give my concerns and fears to You, trusting You will continue to love me and my children, and trusting You will give me the wisdom and strength I need to remain faithful to my calling as a parent and as Your servant. In Jesus' name. Amen.

Parent Pairs

What are your plans to cover the latchkey issues you face as a parent? Are you satisfied that those plans provide a sufficient amount of care and supervision for your teenagers? How often do you pray for your teens' safety and protection? What prayer do you pray when you ask God to protect your teens from harm and danger? How often do you bring your teens to church to experience the anchor of God's grace in an uncertain world?

Read Psalm 121:3–4 and consider the following questions as you discuss the **Parent Pairs** section with your spouse or another parent.

Latchkey Kids

(To be done with your spouse or another parent.)

1. My greatest concern as a latchkey parent is: *(Rank these on a scale of 1 to 10, with 1 being your greatest concern and 10 your least concern.)*

   —— My teens would harm themselves and not know what to do.

   —— There would be long-term harm to the happiness and well-being of my teens.

   —— My teens would not follow my instructions and my home would be ruined.

   —— Other people would perceive me as an inadequate parent.

   —— I would miss the opportunity to interact with my teens when they most need my help, immediately after school.

   —— I would have no control over what my teens did and with whom.

   —— My teens would never do their homework, putting more stress on me when I returned home.

   —— My teens would be bored and feel abandoned.

   —— I wouldn't have any concerns because I would trust my teens.

   —— I could trust my teens implicitly, but I wouldn't be able to trust their friends.

2. As I assess my latchkey situation with my teens, three things I believe I have done well are:

3. As I assess my current latchkey situation with my teens, three things I wish I could change are:

4. My current latchkey plan is:

   a. I return home at _____.

   b. The names and numbers of other significant people in the neighborhood are:

   c. The best way for me to communicate with my teens during this time is _____, and at what time: _____.

   d. The tasks I expect my teens to do before I get home are:

   e. If they get them all done, I usually:

   f. When they don't get them all done, I usually:

   g. My list of who is acceptable in my home, and what is acceptable, is as follows:

   h. If my latch key plan fails, I can fall back upon:

5. Currently, I am satisfied with the way I pray for my teenagers.

    Agree   Disagree

6. In the space provided, write a prayer you might use to daily ask God to protect and care for your teens.

7. The strength I draw from Psalm 121:3–4 is:

I rejoiced with those who said to me,
"Let us go to the house of the LORD."
(Psalm 122:1)

It's Not Sunday

Sundays traditionally have been a day of rest. Early Christians also used Sundays as the day to worship—the day to remember Jesus Christ was raised from the dead as the conqueror over death. Today, Sundays are often neither restful nor worshipful. When families are young, Mom or Dad take the time to get children ready for church, but once in the service, they may fail to hear anything sung or said. Instead, their time will be occupied trying to keep their child quiet enough to keep others from being disturbed as they worship.

By the time that same child reaches middle school and high school, she is old enough to voice her own opinion about church. Unfortunately, by this time church has more than likely become a symbol of her parents' rules and generation. Since the process of breaking away from parents begins in adolescence, it is no wonder that at this time in her life, church and traditional Sunday worship becomes one battleground in the endless struggle for personal power and control.

What's a parent to do? Give in to your teens' request and let them stay home to observe Sunday any way they wish? Or insist they go along? Whatever parents decide, they probably wish the time would come again when they could say with the psalmist, "I rejoiced with those who said to me, 'Let us go into the house of the LORD.'"

As we look back at this Psalm, the passage reflects a time when worship was central in Israel. Families viewed their pilgrimage to Jerusalem as an annual, joyous event. The psalmist also reflects a basic tenet in ancient Israel, grounded in the principle of worship. Humans were created to worship the Lord. When God comes to us in worship, He cleanses us, transforms us through His grace, and empowers us to live out our faith as we use our God-given time, talents, and possessions to serve others.

It is vital that worship be central to our lives today. God comes to us in corporate worship. He is there as we acknowledge our sinfulness and plead for forgiveness. He is there as we hear the Word and partake of the Lord's Supper with the rest of the body of Christ. Worship is an opportunity for each member of our family to be touched by God's grace and to realize that through the gift of our Lord and Savior Jesus Christ, God's grace for us never ends. As God comes to us in corporate worship, we are empowered to live each day in the embrace of that never-ending grace. And when we as parents take the time to participate in weekly worship and have daily devotions with our children, no matter what age they may be, worship becomes one of the main ingredients holding our families together.

I'm not going to church!

My name is Trish. I'm divorced, and the mother of three children: Alyssa, 13; Allen, 11; and Amy, 9. On top of my full-time day job, I work hard every Saturday night as a waitress to make ends meet. Every other weekend, my kids spend time with their father.

When the kids are with their dad, he never expects them to go to church. When they're with me, church is something I expect. In fact, it's something I demand. I've gone so far as to say, "Kids, if you are going to live with me, these are the rules. If you don't like them, you can go live with your father full time as far as I care!"

My hope is they'll never take me up on that offer. The trouble is both Alyssa and Allen are at the age where they're telling me they don't want to go to church. They say it's boring. And Amy is so hard to get going on Sunday morning. So every Sunday it's a battle to get everyone to church. Sometimes we end up not speaking to one another while we're there. It's really embarrassing.

Sometimes I want to give up trying. I think everyone should be happy when they go to church, not mad. What should I do?

What would you do?

- How might Trish's concerns be different if she lived with the father of her children?

- Trish says, "church is something I demand." How might she be sending the wrong message about church to her three children?

- Trish thinks everyone should be happy when they go to church. What do you think? What might be the proper mood with which to enter church?

- What would be the most helpful thing for Trish to do in this situation?

- What would be the most harmful thing for Trish to do?

- What could you suggest to Trish to help her change her situation, and appreciate worship as the opportunity to be in that place where God comes to us in His love and mercy?

Conflict within a family is normal, but when the conflict is about attending worship, the conflict itself seems almost sacrilegious. As a result, most families will give in to the protests of teens rather than make an issue out of their worship attendance. Before we are tempted to give in, however, we might use the potential of conflict with our teens to help us examine our own worship patterns, including our personal devotional life.

- Are we giving the message that we are fed and renewed through worship, or that we attend only as an obligation? Teens are usually quick studies of their parents' actions and attitudes. They are able to tell if worship is a central part of our life, or if we're simply going through the motions. They will take their cue from us, and emulate our attitudes and behavior.

- Is worship the center from which everything else in our life proceeds, or is it an afterthought, something we do because we have no other scheduled appointments? If we consider worship to be the center of our life, sooner or later our teens may consider worship the center of their lives, especially when they are not as easily influenced by their peers' ideas about church and other religious matters.

- Is prayer an important part of our lives? How often do we pray with and for our teens? If weekly corporate worship, personal prayer, and family devotions have not been part of our history, it's never too late to start. We might begin by singing a hymn, praying a psalm, or reinstating the common table prayer as a part of our mealtimes, or simply communicating to our teens that we pray for them daily.

When our children see that worship is our connection to the Lord—where He comes to us and we are given opportunities to respond to the gifts of His grace—they too will come to see its importance and the power of God's transformation in our lives. If conflicts continue, they can be used as opportunities to grow in our faith toward God and in our love for one another, and through the power of the Holy Spirit, trust that God will help us along the way.

Closing Prayer

O God, I thank You for giving me the Sabbath day as a day where I can come into Your presence and be claimed as Your own. Help my Sabbath observance become central to my life. Move my teens to see You as the center of their lives. As they do, help them discover the joy of a life of worship and experience anew the gifts of Your grace. In Jesus' name. Amen.

Parent Pairs

Is worship a source of conflict with your teens, or is it an opportunity for joy? How do you address the issue of worship practices with your teens? How do your own worship practices affect your expectations of your teens' worship practices?

Read Psalm 122:1 and consider the following questions as you discuss the **Parent Pairs** section with your spouse or another parent.

It's Not Sunday

(To be done with your spouse or another parent.)

1. When it comes to my worship attendance, I go: *(You may choose more than one answer.)*

   ❑ Every week.

   ❑ When nothing else gets in the way of going to church.

   ❑ On holidays and holy days.

   ❑ I haven't graced the door of a church since I was confirmed.

2. When I attend a worship service at my home church, I: *(You may choose more than one answer.)*

   ❑ Leave refreshed, renewed, and strengthened for the week to come.

   ❑ Receive and rejoice in God's love and forgiveness.

   ❑ Find my thoughts wandering, usually to tasks I've yet to complete.

   ❑ Always find it difficult to stay awake.

3. When it comes to my teens' worship attendance, I believe: *(You may choose more than one answer.)*

   ❑ They should attend each week.

   ❑ My role as a parent should be to give my teens a taste of what worship is like.

   ❑ It's okay for my teens to miss, especially if they have something important to go to on a Sunday morning.

   ❑ It's all right for them to attend only on holidays or holy days.

4. When my teens experience worship, I hope they: *(You may choose more than once answer.)*

   ❑ Leave refreshed, renewed, and strengthened for the week to come.

   ❑ Have experienced God's love and forgiveness.

   ❑ Know it is all right for their thoughts to wander.

   ❑ I have no expectations of my teens.

5. My teens and I struggle over their church attendance.

   Agree   Disagree

6. Three things I have tried to do to encourage my teens to go to worship have been:

7. These three things were helpful because:

8. These three things were harmful because:

9. If I were to do things differently concerning my teens and their worship attendance, I would:

10. If I were to give one piece of advice to my friends who were struggling with their teens about worship attendance, it would be:

11. If I were to rate my personal devotional life, I would say: (*You may choose more than one answer.*)

    ☐ It really keeps me going each day.

    ☐ I wish I were more faithful.

    ☐ It is almost non-existent.

    ☐ It's something I'd like to start.

12. My plan to start my daily devotions would include:

13. I plan to start my daily devotions by *(include the date and regular time):*

14. I will share my plan with my teens.

   Agree   **Disagree**

15. The strength I draw from Psalm 122:1 is:

Brothers, I do not consider myself yet to
have taken hold of it. But one thing I do:
Forgetting what is behind and straining
toward what is ahead, I press on toward the
goal to win the prize for which God has
called me heavenward in Christ Jesus.
(Philippians 3:13–14)

Put Me in Coach

Sports are a large part of our culture, so it's no
wonder they often become an integral part of teens'—and parents'—lives.
Participation is often limited only by the amount of money the parents are willing to spend as they seek to involve their teens in a wide variety of sports and
other activities. Traditional stereotypes have even been cast aside, opening up
basketball, hockey, tennis, dance, soccer, baseball, softball, figure skating, and so
many other activities to girls and boys of all ages.

When we parents allow our teenagers to participate in these activities, we also
trust that the adults who work with our teens will be responsible and will impart
needed values and lessons not only about the sport, but about life as well. So what
kind of adult role models do we seek for our teenagers? What values and lessons
do we hope our teens will learn from their activities that will transfer to other
areas of their lives?

Trouble and conflict erupt when we fail to communicate to our teens' coaches the wishes and desires we have for our teens, and the values we wish them to
live by. The more clearly we are able to identify those wishes, desires, and values to our teens and their coaches, the greater the likelihood our teens will have
a positive experience from and will grow as a result of their participation in that
sport.

The challenge for us as Christian parents is not to use sports only as an opportunity for our teenagers to remain active or stay out of trouble. Instead, we can use the experience to help our teens see the non-physical benefits of sports participation—discipline and faithfulness—and translate both to their walk with God and their journey of faith, which began at their Baptism. Their faith journey will be filled with obstacles, but they can use the experience and endurance gained from sports to realize God gives them the strength and commitment to continue their journey of faith, trusting that as they do, He travels with them.

I can't say that here!

I'm Sam. I'm 14, and the starting point guard for my freshman basketball team. We're a great team; we've been playing together for almost four years. I love basketball, and I hope I can play it in college. The only problem is, I can't stand my coach. In fact, I hate him.

Whenever the pressure is on, or whenever I make a mistake, he swears at me. Actually he swears at the whole team. It's not that I'm all that religious. It's just that when he does it, I feel less than human. I'm afraid he'd bench me if I told him that the way he uses language is just plain stupid.

My parents know all about his language problem, and they plan to talk to our athletic director. But if they do, I think I'd probably die right there on the spot.

What would you do?

- How realistic is Sam's story? What would make most 14-year-olds do nothing when their coach uses offensive language?

- What are Sam's choices as he reacts to his coach?

- What is Sam's most helpful choice?

- What is Sam's most harmful choice?

- What kind of support do you believe Sam wants from his parents?

- Sam, like any other 14-year-old, claims he will "probably die right there on the spot" if his parents talk to the athletic director. What do you believe Sam's parents should do? How involved should parents become in a sport or activity once their son or daughter reaches the middle or high school years?

- How could Sam's faith help him endure?

- How can Sam's parents be the most helpful for him as he plays for a coach he doesn't like?

Before enrolling teenagers in any program, ask:

- Why am I enrolling my teen in this particular program at this particular time?

- What is it that I want for my teen by his or her participation in this program?

- At the end of his or her time in the program, what do I want my teen to have learned?

- What is it that my teen wants from the program?

- In relationship to all my other expenses, can I afford to have my teen participating in this program?

Even as we ask ourselves these questions, consider the relationship athletics have to the rest of our teens' lives. Popular slogans proclaim, "[This sport] is life, the rest is just details." As Christian parents, our main message to our children is that Jesus Christ brings new life, and through that transformation, the details of our lives take on new meaning and new purpose. As we focus on Jesus as the center of our family's life, we remember that He came not to be served, but to serve and give His life as a ransom for us. Sports, as well as all our other activities, become a way to use God-given talents in the unique setting where He has placed us for a time, and for the benefit of those around us.

All too often, we allow our teenagers to participate in athletics or other extra-curricular activities simply because we believe it will be good for them. Sometimes we allow them to participate without taking into consideration the long-range cost of that participation emotionally on our teens and financially to our own pocketbooks. Asking questions and hearing answers can be difficult for us and our teens, but once we ask the difficult questions about our teens' participation, we can be more confident the program we select accomplishes the goals we desire for them. And throughout the process, we can depend on the grace of God to guide us as we seek the answers to our questions and the outcome of our goals, ultimately for the benefit of our teenagers.

Closing Prayer

Gracious God, You created my teens and have allowed them to grow in wisdom and strength. Help me as their parent to help them make choices beneficial to their emotional growth as well as their physical growth, that as they exercise their bodies, their lives might reflect the wonders of Your glory and the gift of Your love. For Jesus' sake. Amen.

Parent Pairs

What role do athletics play in the life of your teens? In the rest of your family? What are the values you want displayed in those who coach your children? How balanced is your life? Are athletics becoming a god in your life, displacing worship of the Triune God as your family's center?

Read Philippians 3:13–14 and consider the following questions as you discuss the **Parent Pairs** section with your spouse or another parent.

Put Me in Coach

(To be done with your spouse or another parent.)

1. My teens participate in the following after-school activities:

2. My goal of allowing my teens to participate in these activities is: *(You may choose more than one answer.)*

   ❏ To learn skills that will help them become more successful as adults.

   ❏ To keep them as busy as possible so they will stay out of trouble.

   ❏ To help them continue on a path that could lead to an athletic or performing scholarship.

   ❏ To make new friends.

   ❏ To allow them to pursue their interests.

   ❏ To encourage my children to continue to step out of their area of comfort and expand their horizons.

3. My teens' goal as they participate in these activities is: *(You may choose more than one answer.)*

   ❏ To have fun.

   ❏ To develop a skill that might ultimately give them an athletic or performing scholarship.

   ❏ To make new friends.

   ❏ To pursue their interests.

   ❏ To be with their friends.

   ❏ To be the best they possibly can be at what they have chosen.

   ❏ My teens have no goals.

4. As I look at the activities in which my teens are involved, their lives seem: (*You may choose more than one answer.*)

☐ Extremely balanced.

☐ Out of balance and out of control.

☐ In and out of control depending on the season.

☐ Centered on Jesus Christ.

5. If I could change one thing about my teens' extracurricular involvement so their life would be more centered, it would be:

6. The kind of adult I believe should be involved with my teens in an after-school activity should be someone who: (*You may choose more than one answer.*)

☐ Is a parent of a teen involved with the program.

☐ Is familiar with the program but has no teens involved with the program.

☐ Is more interested in the development of the individuals within the program instead of overall program results.

☐ Is concerned about placing my teens in a situation where they can succeed.

☐ Is not concerned about what parents think of him or her.

☐ Has a strong moral character and is be able to communicate his or her values to the members of the program.

☐ Is concerned only with winning and winning performances.

7. As I look over the above characteristics, and as I consider the adults involved with my teens' after-school activities, I would rate them: (*Circle one.*)

Superior   Above average   Average

Poor   Not even close to my ideal

58

8. Make a list of the significant adults involved with your teens in extra-curricular programs. Write down their strengths as well as their weaknesses.

Coach or leader	Activity	Strengths	Weaknesses

9. After evaluating the significant adults in my children's after-school programs, I find myself *(Circle one.)* **satisfied/dissatisfied** with the way these adults interact in my teens' lives.

10. After evaluating the significant adults in my teens' after-school programs, I find I need to address some concerns with one or more of the adults.

   Agree   Disagree

11. Write down your concerns and the way you plan to address those concerns.

   My concerns

   My plan to address those concerns

12. The limit to the expenses I pay for my teens' extracurricular activities is:

   _____

13. The strength I draw from Philippians 3:13–14 is:

But grow in the grace and knowledge of our
Lord and Savior Jesus Christ. To Him be
glory both now and forever! Amen.
(2 Peter 3:18)

Making the Grade

Once children reach school age, they will
spend more time in school than they do at home. As a result, their school activities, teachers, and grades all have an incredible impact on what they will do and
who they will be in the future. Parents may find it difficult to communicate to
their children—especially their teens—the importance of working hard *now* for
the betterment of their future. But in most cases, good grades mean a better
chance for good scholarships and job opportunities, while poor grades limit both
school and career choices.

So what are parents to do? The question can be extremely difficult if our
teenagers, instead of being highly self-motivated, need supervision and limits
imposed on them to stay on task and complete their work successfully. In the end,
our teens need to complete school on their own, by their own merit. That's why
we need God's help in this all-encompassing process.

In the midst of concerns about making daily or yearly grades, parents need to
emphasize that learning is a lifelong process. As Christians, we are called to grow
continually in God's grace and in the knowledge of our Lord and Savior Jesus
Christ. So while it is important that our teens learn world history, algebra, and
English, it is also important that they learn—and continually study—what God has
done for them through Jesus Christ, His Son. This learning process, which began

in the waters of our Baptism, will continue throughout our lives until we are reunited with our Father in heaven. Then, as St. Paul states in 1 Corinthians 13:12, "Now [we] know in part; then [we] shall know fully, even as [we are] fully known."

I'm tired of good grades!

My name is Shelly. I'm the parent of two teenage kids. Sarah is 18. She always has been highly motivated. She's never received anything less than a B+ on her report card, and I think she only has had two B+s her whole academic career. Sam, who is 16, is quite a different story.

He used to get good grades in middle school, and I was so proud of him. But now that he's in high school, he's on the football team and has been dating Cindy quite regularly for the last five months. Since then, his grades have dropped—dropped dramatically. He's gone from As and Bs to Cs and Ds. I've talked to him about it, but I don't get very far.

Just yesterday, we were talking about it again when he said to me, "Mom, I'm tired of you wanting me to get good grades in every subject. I've decided I'm only going to get good grades in the subjects I like!"

When I asked him what subjects those were, he just shrugged my question off and said, "I don't know, Mom. Maybe I'll get married after high school and then go to a trade school!" When I heard that, I didn't know what to say. I still don't know how to respond. I just wish someone would help me!

What would you do?

- Before you react to the situation, what other information about Sam and his grades, would you like to have?

- If you were Shelly, how would you respond?

- Say Shelly came to you, her best friend, for your sage advice. What would you say to her to help her deal with Sam?

- Imagine that Sam came to you with complaints about his interfering, overbearing mother, who is your best friend. What might you say to Sam to help him see both sides of the issue?

- If Shelly does nothing, what is the worst possible thing that could happen to Sam?

- If you were Shelly, what could you do or would you be willing to do to prevent that from happening?

As tiring as it may be for parents, studies have shown the more involved they are in the education of their children, the more successful their children will be—not only in school, but later in life as well. As we continue to parent our teens through the middle and high school years, there are things we can do to help them so we not only live together in peace, but continue to learn together, and through learning, grow together. Consider the following:

- Remind your teens they are accountable to their teacher, to themselves, and to you. As a result, never forget to ask three basic questions: "Do you have any homework? Have you completed it? Can I look it over?" This may seem elementary, especially for those who believe teenagers should be accountable to themselves. However, the more our teens realize we want to view the homework, the less the chance there will be a breakdown in their academic work.

- Be enthusiastic about learning. Even if you can't always remember the details, be enthusiastic about the days when you were in school as well. Teens who sense their parents like learning will be far less likely to avoid or dislike education.

- Model by what you do in everyday life that you enjoy learning—not just a select academic menu, but anything that aids your spirit of discovery.

- Be willing to set and follow through with consequences if grades fail to improve.

- Remember that God leads us in a lifelong process of learning who we are as His adopted, redeemed, and forgiven children. Bring your teens to the weekly touch point of God's grace through worship. Encourage them as they grow in grace and in knowledge of their Lord and Savior Jesus Christ. Help them discover that in the joy of knowing more about God and His will for them, He will help them discover more about themselves, and more about the miracle of God's grace that helps all believers understand the unconditional power of God's love and forgiveness through Jesus Christ, our Lord.

Closing Prayer

Loving God, teach my teens how to confess their sins and lead them to the place where they will experience forgiveness and be empowered to learn and grow in the grace and knowledge of their Lord and Savior Jesus Christ. In Jesus' name. Amen.

Parent Pairs

How much pressure to make good grades do your teens experience? How frustrated do you become with your teens' ability or inability to learn? How do you encourage your teens to grow in the grace and knowledge of their Lord and Savior Jesus Christ? How have you as their parent taken the time to be nurtured in your own faith?

Read 2 Peter 3:18 and consider the following questions as you discuss the **Parent Pairs** section with your spouse or another parent.

Making the Grade

(To be done with your spouse or another parent.)

1. The grades students receive are a strong indication of how successful they will be later in life.

1	2	3	4	5	6	7	8	9	10

   Strongly Agree   Agree   Not Sure   Disagree   Strongly Disagree

2. The more pressure put on students to receive good grades, the more negatively they will react to that pressure.

1	2	3	4	5	6	7	8	9	10

   Strongly Agree   Agree   Not Sure   Disagree   Strongly Disagree

3. I would be willing to do anything to get my teens to receive good grades, including paying them for each good grade they receive.

1	2	3	4	5	6	7	8	9	10

   Strongly Agree   Agree   Not Sure   Disagree   Strongly Disagree

4. I don't care what kind of grades my teens receive as long as they are happy in life.

1	2	3	4	5	6	7	8	9	10

   Strongly Agree   Agree   Not Sure   Disagree   Strongly Disagree

5. It is important for my teens to do the best they possibly can in every subject.

1	2	3	4	5	6	7	8	9	10

   Strongly Agree   Agree   Not Sure   Disagree   Strongly Disagree

6. I think it is important for my teens to do the best they possibly can only in the subjects they like.

1	2	3	4	5	6	7	8	9	10

Strongly Agree   Agree   Not Sure   Disagree   Strongly Disagree

7. I do not expect my son or daughter to go to college, as long as he or she has some post-high school education.

1	2	3	4	5	6	7	8	9	10

Strongly Agree   Agree   Not Sure   Disagree   Strongly Disagree

8. Good grades do not prove who is intelligent; they only prove who can give the answers the teacher wants.

1	2	3	4	5	6	7	8	9	10

Strongly Agree   Agree   Not Sure   Disagree   Strongly Disagree

9. In the space below, choose the statements from above with which you agree and discuss the reason for your agreement.

10. In the space below choose the statements from above with which you disagree and discuss the reason for your disagreement.

11. In the space below choose the statements from above about which you might be uncertain and discuss the reason for your uncertainty.

12. I participate in my teens' education by:

13. I participate in my teens' faith education by:

14. The strength I draw from 2 Peter 3:18 is:

Nor did we eat anyone's food without paying for it. On the contrary, we worked night and day, laboring and toiling so that we would not be a burden to any of you.
(2 Thessalonians 3:8)

Who Needs to Work?

One goal of parenting is to make sure children can provide for themselves in such a way that they are not dependent on their parents when they are older. As a result, when teens begin their first job, both teens and their parents are happy. Troubles arise, however, when the job takes center stage and everything else falls by the wayside.

For the apostles, work was a means to an end. It gave them the money to eat and pay for shelter, but by no means gave them their identity. Instead, their identity came from their call to be followers of Jesus. Their primary job was to invite others to follow Jesus as they carried the Gospel message to all ends of the earth. We who are parents of teens need to help them remember that work is not the source of identity. We are not identified nor valued by God because of what we do; we are identified and valued by God because of what God has done for us through our Lord and Savior Jesus Christ.

It is important for teens to gain work experience and have the satisfaction of earning their own money and making their own contribution to the benefit of society. On the other hand, teens have the rest of their lives to work; working now can rob them of the freedom they have to still be who they really are: growing children. How do we as parents help our teens maintain a balance between their work and the formation of their identity?

Unfortunately, teenagers all too often believe they are invincible. As a result, they initially have no problem committing to everything, yet never have enough time to do what they need to do. As parents, we need to gently remind our teens that they are not limitless. We need to teach them there are more things in life than money. We can also serve to help them remember their center, Jesus Christ, and help them recognize that in the midst of all their commitments, their God, who remains committed to them, invites them to a life of commitment and service in His kingdom.

It's only 15 hours a week!

Marlys was a star swimmer on her high school swimming team. She got up every morning at 5:00 A.M. to swim extra laps before school and swam every day after school for two hours—all before the season even had begun. During the season, with meets during the week, Marlys was swimming whenever and wherever she could, as long as she could.

On the other hand, Marlys wanted to get a part-time job. She planned to go to college and also wanted to buy a car, since both her parents worked and needed both family cars. One day Char, her best friend, said, "Marlys, there's an opening for someone to help out in the pharmacy where I work. It would be the perfect job for you. It's only weekends—eight hours on Saturday and seven hours on Sunday." Although she knew her parents would be opposed, she went ahead and interviewed for the job. She was hired on the spot.

When Marlys came home that evening, she said to her parents, "Mom, Dad, I just got hired by Beaseley's Pharmacy. The best part about it is that they only want me for 15 hours a week, just on Saturday and Sunday."

"You what?" both parents exclaimed.

"Marlys," her mother continued, "you never have enough time to do everything you want to do now! How will you have time for anything at school, including swimming, when you're working all the time?"

Marlys turned and counted to 10. Then she faced her parents and said, "...

What would you do?

- If you were Marlys's parents, and were trying logically and unemotionally to explain your concerns to her, what would you say?

- From her parents' perspective what do you believe could be the best possible outcome of her taking this job? What do you believe could be the worst possible outcome?

- From Marlys's point of view, what do you believe could be the best possible outcome of her taking this job? What do you believe could be the worst possible outcome?

- Now that you have thought about possible outcomes, finish the conversation between Marlys and her parents.

- If you were the parents in this situation, on what would you base your decision that this job would not benefit Marlys?

- If Marlys is stressed about money, cars, and college, what might her parents do to relieve her stress and address her concerns?

As we discuss the subject of working teens, we have to realize that work does contribute to self-esteem. As a result, not only do teens want the money, they need to be placed into situations where they are contributing to the welfare of their society and the betterment of their world. At the same time, however, we need to remind our teens that their worth is not intrinsically tied to what they do. Esteem involves more than that; it means God has adopted our teens as His sons and daughters, and this adoption as God's children gives them their value as workers in His kingdom. We can tell our teens they can make a difference in any situation they find themselves, whether on the job or not, for God has already made a difference in them because of Jesus Christ.

Teenagers need to feel they are making a difference, but we don't have to wait until they are employed to convey to them our sense of their importance. As parents, we need to relate to our teenagers each day to help them feel wanted, needed, and valued as God's children and as a valued part of society so they might realize first and foremost they make a difference in the home in which they live, as well as in the kingdom of God.

Closing Prayer

Gracious God, from the beginning of creation You called upon us to work on this earth. As my teens begin to enter the work force, give them a sense of balance and an understanding of their limitations. Help them understand that no matter what they do, they remain valuable in Your sight, and no matter how anxious they might be about their future, You have promised to provide for them always. In Jesus' name. Amen.

Parent Pairs

What are your current expectations about your teens working? How many hours do you want your teens to work? How important is work in relationship to your teens' grades? In what ways do you help your teens see they are valued children of God, outside of their participation in the workforce? How do you want your teens' work experience to help them prepare for life after school?

Read 2 Thessalonians 3:8 and consider the following questions as you discuss the **Parent Pairs** section with your spouse or another parent.

Who Needs to Work?

(To be done with your spouse or another parent.)

1. Listed below are age groups of adolescents. For each group, write the average number of hours per day you would expect them to work during school and during summer vacation.

Ages:	School Night	School Weekend	Summer Vacation
13–15:	_____	_____	_____
15–17:	_____	_____	_____
17–19:	_____	_____	_____

2. As my teens get older: *(You may choose more than one answer.)*
   - ❑ I believe they need to make a greater contribution to the household through their work.
   - ❑ I believe the main purpose for their working is to save money for college.
   - ❑ I think working is only valuable because it gives them a taste of what the "real" world is like.
   - ❑ I'm not all that concerned whether my teens work.

3. If my teens get a job: *(You may choose more than one answer.)*
   - ❑ They had better make sure nothing else in their life suffers, especially school work.
   - ❑ I don't care what happens as long as they like what they do.
   - ❑ I need to approve the kind of job they get.
   - ❑ I trust they will better understand all the dynamics of the working world.

4. My teens currently have a job:

Agree   Disagree

5. My teens' current jobs have helped them in the following three ways.

6. My teens' current jobs have harmed them in the following three ways.

7. If I could share one concern about my teens' working, I would say to them:

8. I had a job as a teenager:

Agree   Disagree

9. Having a job helped me by:

10. Having a job harmed me by:

11. If it weren't for my teens' jobs, they wouldn't know what to do.

Agree   Disagree

12. My teens' jobs keep them out of trouble.

   Agree   Disagree

13. My teens' jobs contribute to their self-esteem.

   Agree   Disagree

14. I try to develop my teens' identity as children of God and their value in God's sight by:

15. The three most important characteristics I value in my teens, whether or not they work, are:

16. The strength I draw from 2 Thessalonians 3:8 is:

Greater love has no one than this, that
he lay down his life for his friends. You are
My friends if you do what I command.
(John 15:13–14)

They're My Friends

There's no getting around it: the world of adolescents begins and ends with friends. By the time adolescents reach the age of 13 or 14, their primary allegiance shifts from their family to their friends. As this shift occurs, many a mother and father cast a wary eye on the type of company their son or daughter keeps.

The shift from family to friends is normal, and in most cases healthy. However, when we as parents don't approve of our teens' friends, conflict occurs. Sometimes our fears are unjustified. Other times, however, our fears are realized as the influence of friends leads our teens down roads destructive both now and in the future. What's a parent to do? We want to give our teens room to make their own decisions—including who their friends are, but too often they fail to realize decisions made now can affect them the rest of their lives, sometimes to the point of serious injury or death.

Unfortunately, our fears that our teens may waste away their future, or worse—that we might bury them—are all too realistic. Our only hope lies in knowing that in the midst of our fears, we can be assured God listens to us, God agonizes with us, and God keeps watch over our sons and daughters at all times, even when we ourselves cannot.

As we deal with our teens and their friends, we need to remind them that when all is said and done, there is one true Friend who has honored us by calling us *His* friends even when we do not treat Him as *our* friend. As the gospel of John proclaims, "Greater love has no one than this, that he lay down his life for his friends." Of course, we parents need to be reminded that Jesus not only calls our teens to be friends, but that He calls us friends as well. This friendship that God establishes with us through His Son, Jesus Christ, is confirmed over and over again as we receive His body and blood. It will give us strength, comfort, and hope as we deal with our teens and their friends.

We're afraid we've lost him!

My name is Kathy. I'm the mother of three sons: Greg is 16, Ben is 14, and Michael is 12. My husband Rich and I both work, and we have to work hard to make ends meet. Our boys have been a joy for both of us all these years, so I really shouldn't complain, but I want to tell you that I'm scared.

Greg was always a neat, outgoing kid. He had plenty of friends, friends that Rich and I both liked and accepted into our home. But in the last year, things have changed. Greg has changed. He has changed friends, his hair, his clothes style. He has even changed the way he talks to us and to his brothers. He isn't as outgoing as he once was. His grades have begun to slip, and he spends a lot of time just sitting in his room, listening to CDs.

It all started when this new boy, Kyle, came to Greg's school. When Greg brought him home, I thought, "They're as different as night from day!" But I didn't say anything to Greg. Now I hear from other parents that Kyle has so many problems, and there are even rumors Kyle does drugs. I know for a fact that Kyle has run away from home on more than one occasion. I feel so helpless. Rich and I feel so helpless. It's like we've lost our son, and we don't know what to do.

What would you do?

- What other information would be helpful for you to know before you respond to the situation?

- What signs does Greg exhibit that give Kathy a good reason to be concerned?

- We know nothing about Greg's father, Rich. What role do you believe Rich has played in this situation, or should play from now on?

- If Kathy came to you for advice, what would you say to her that might give her hope?

- When Greg brought Kyle home, Kathy said nothing. What might Kathy have said initially to Greg about Kyle?

- Pretend you are a friend of the family, an adult who has been significant in Greg's past. What would you say to Greg about your concerns? How would you approach the situation?

Life isn't easy when the friends our teenagers choose are not the friends we would choose for them. At times it may feel we are walking on eggshells; trying to be accepting and affirming of our teens' choice of friends, but firmly believing in our authority to intervene before the newly formed relationship proves to be as harmful to our teens as we fear.

As parents, we need to realize our fears and feelings are valid. Our challenge is to listen to our fears, learn from them, then try to communicate what we feel to our teens without threatening them or making them believe we are judging or condemning them for choices they have made.

As a result, we need to do a lot of listening, especially to what our teens desire. Asking questions such as, "Tell me more about Kyle, his parents, his interests," indicate we are willing to listen first, and perhaps judge later. Continuing conversations with, "I can see you and Kyle like each other. What do you share in common? What is it about Kyle that you like?" shows we are genuinely interested in the relationships our teens are forming. At the same time, we can point out changes in their behavior that seem troubling in a non-threatening way with comments such as, "Greg, I see you're spending a lot of time in your room lately. You just need to know that your dad and I like seeing you. You are an important part of this family!" Our respect will help our teens respect us, as well as any opinions we may share with them.

The wonderful thing about parenting is every situation helps us learn more—especially about ourselves and our teens. And as we learn more, God will continue to bless us with His abundant love and never-ending support through Jesus, our best Friend. No matter our situation, we can gain strength from knowing this Friend cares for us so much He did indeed lay down His life for us, for our teens, and for their friends as well.

Closing Prayer

O God of youth, stir my parental heart so I might have compassion and love for my teenagers and be patient with their choice of friends. At the same time, remind me that You have given me Your Son, Jesus Christ, my Lord, who became my Savior and Friend, and showed His great love for me by laying down His life for my salvation. In His name. Amen.

Parent Pairs

Do you like all your teens' friends? As you think about your teens' friends, what are the characteristics that make them good friends? What personality traits might make them questionable or harmful friends? What situations in your life have led you to believe that Jesus truly is your best Friend?

Read John 15:13–14 and consider the following questions as you discuss the **Parent Pairs** section with your spouse or another parent.

They're My Friends

(To be done with your spouse or another parent.)

1. I like all my teens' friends.

    Agree   **Disagree**

2. On a scale of 1 to 10, with 1 being the most important and 10 the least, rank the kind of person you would seek if you were to find friends for your teens.

    _____ They come from similar family backgrounds.

    _____ They are motivated to do well in school.

    _____ They have the same interests as my teens.

    _____ They like to have a good time.

    _____ They have definite goals for the future.

    _____ They believe in God.

    _____ They go to church regularly.

    _____ They treat their parents with respect.

    _____ They can be trusted by me and my teens.

    _____ They are loyal.

3. Now imagine your teens answered the same question. What would their list look like?

    _____ They come from similar family backgrounds.

    _____ They are motivated to do well in school.

    _____ They have the same interests as myself.

    _____ They like to have a good time.

    _____ They have definite goals for the future.

    _____ They believe in God.

    _____ They go to church regularly.

_____ They treat their parents with respect.

_____ They can be trusted by me and my parents.

_____ They are loyal.

4. Three similarities I see as I compare the lists are:

5. Three differences I see as I contrast the lists are:

6. As I look at the similarities and the differences in the lists, two things I would like to change as I deal with my teens' friends whom I dislike might be:

7. My greatest fear as I think about my teens' friends is:

8. If I could give some advice to other parents who don't like their teens' friends, it would be:

9. Jesus claimed me as His friend by:

10. Knowing that Jesus has claimed me as His friend helps when I deal with my teens' friends by:

11. The strength I draw from John 15:13–14 is:

If I say, "Surely the darkness will hide me
and the light become night around me,"
even the darkness will not be dark to You;
the night will shine like the day, for darkness is as light to You. (Psalm 139:11–12)

It's Not That Late

As our children reach their teenage years, one
particularly controversial topic always seems to take center stage in discussions:
curfew. As they become older and more independent, our teens want to go out
more often and stay out later each time. For us parents, it makes no difference
whether they are on dates or in large groups, the later the hour, the greater the
worry for us. Of course, the greater the worry for us parents, the greater the stress
for our sons and daughters.

At stake for most parents is the safety of their teenagers. Statistics will bear out
that a person's chances of being hit and killed by a drunken driver increase sig-
nificantly after 10:00 P.M., and go up even more dramatically after 1:00 A.M. If
teens are out alone with someone of the opposite sex, parents' concerns about the
sexual activities of their teens increase as well.

Although teenagers use this time to stake claims for their independence, moth-
ers, fathers, stepmothers, and stepfathers use this time to express their fears for
the future of their children. Parents do not want to see their teens put themselves
at risk; parents do not want to bury their own children. Curfews and limits need
to be established not only for the safety and well-being of teenagers, but also for
the peace and serenity of the parents.

The psalmist in Psalm 139 talks about the intricate knowledge God, our Father, possesses about us. The same God who created both night and day, who set limits between the heavens and the earth, and between the earth and the seas, cares for us and loves us. This Psalm reminds us that no matter where our teens are, God goes with them. As our teens stretch their boundaries and test their limits, God continues to be with them and love them. They always remain His precious children.

As concerns about time and activities surface, it is helpful for us as parents to remember that God is *our* parent. He is willing to bear our worries and shoulder our concerns. For all of us who are concerned about things that go bump in the night, as the psalmist writes, even the darkness is not dark to God.

At what time?

It was the day of Phil's senior prom. Phil had been dating Cindy for more than a year, and they had made big plans and spent quite a bit of money getting ready for the big night. As Phil began to get ready that evening, his mom, Elaine, came into his room for a conversation.

"Phil, tell me about the plans you and Cindy have for the prom," she started.

"Well," Phil replied. "First we're going to the promenade in the city park, then we've made reservations for dinner at the Cottonwood at Silver City. Then of course there's the dance. After that, Mark is having a party at his parents' cabin. I don't plan to be home until some time late Saturday morning, then some of us are going boating on the river Saturday afternoon."

Elaine frowned. "I don't want you and Cindy to go to Mark's cabin. It's too late; you wouldn't get there until after 1:00 A.M. and I just don't trust who's driving at that time of night. I'd rather you just bring Cindy back here, rent some videos, then get a little more sleep for Saturday afternoon."

"No way, Mom!" Phil said. "I'm going to Mark's party."

"I don't think so, Phil. Especially not if you want a car to drive ..."

What would you do?

• What additional information might Elaine have tried to discover before making her decision about Phil and Cindy going to Mark's party? Could she have picked a better time to have this conversation?

• What are the options for Phil and his mother to consider as they try to resolve this conflict?

- Elaine appears to agree to no other position but her own. What is the greatest harm if Elaine refuses to negotiate? for Elaine? for Phil? for Cindy?

- What reasons might you give supporting Elaine's decision, and her refusal to change her mind?

- Elaine gives us no idea what a reasonable time for returning from a prom might be. What do you believe is a reasonable time for Phil to return?

- What would happen if Elaine asked Phil for some input in setting a time limit for his return from the prom?

Time moves painfully slow when we find ourselves lying awake in the middle of the night wondering and worrying about what our teens are doing and when they will return. Unfortunately, the answer is not simply to lock them in the house at all times. Not only do they need sunlight, they also need the chance to grow independently of us. Instead, we can use curfews, limitations, and rules in much the same way God uses His commandments for us: providing structure and a means of accountability as a sign of our love for them.

We as parents do have the right to expect our teens to abide by our established limits. We as parents do have the right to expect our teens to show us they are as concerned with our feelings and expectations as much as they are their own. We as parents do have the right to expect our teens to convince us they will not place themselves or others in harmful or risky situations. But we as parents also have the opportunity to be loving and merciful to them—just as the Lord is to us.

How often do we push against the restraints God sets in place for our protection? How often do we fight to be independent of His loving control? How often do we stray into situations that might cause our heavenly Father to catch His breath in worry for our welfare? Yet in His mercy, God forgives us. We are not free from the consequences of our actions, but we are assured of His continuous love for us. Because of this love, we can forgive and love our teens as they continue to explore their world.

The opportunity to parent our teens is an opportunity for us to grow stronger in our relationship with God. We can remember that in the midst of the darkness of night as we wait for our teens to return home, the God who created both darkness and light waits with us. The God who established limits for the sea, the earth, and the heavens will help us as we struggle with the limits we attempt to establish for our teens. The God who has adopted us as His own, reaches out in forgiveness through Christ's body and blood and offers absolution for the time when we stretch *His* limits. And even on the worst of our sleepless nights, we need never fear being alone, for we have a constant companion in our God who never slumbers nor sleeps.

Closing Prayer

O God, protect me from sleepless, worry-filled nights in which I experience anxiety about the safety of my teenagers. Help me realize that just as You set limits upon Your children by giving us the Ten Commandments, so You will strengthen me to continue to set limits on my teenagers. Help me also to realize that even when they are out of my control, You will never take Your eye from them. In Your Son's name. Amen.

Parent Pairs

What are accepted curfews for your teens? As your teens grow older, how do those times change? Do you have clear consequences for your teens if they come home late? Do your teens have any input into the consequences they must face if they come home late? Have you clearly communicated to your teens the reason you want them to have set time limits? How does God help you as you deal with these issues?

Read Psalm 139:11–12 and consider the following questions as you discuss the **Parent Pairs** section with your spouse or another parent.

It's Not That Late

(To be done with your spouse or another parent.)

1. Listed below are different age groups of adolescents. For each age group, write the ideal time you would expect them home, given the day and season.

Ages:	School Night	School Weekend	Summer Night	Summer Weekend
13-15:	_____	_____	_____	_____
15-17:	_____	_____	_____	_____
17-19:	_____	_____	_____	_____

2. How much of a grace period do your teens have before you impose a consequence? Under what circumstances would you allow them to stay out later than the imposed time limit?

3. Write the consequences you would give your teens if they went beyond the grace period or abused the special circumstances.

4. My teens know the consequences if they stay out beyond the designated time I have established.

   Agree   Disagree

5. I have explained to my teens my reason for establishing a designated time for them to return home.

   Agree   Disagree

6. The most effective consequence when my teens have stayed out beyond the designated time has been:

7. The least effective consequence when my teens have stayed out beyond the designated time has been:

8. If I could change one thing about the way I have set time limits on my teens, it would be:

9. My teens have had significant input and ownership of the time limits that have been set for them.

   Agree   Disagree

10. I believe teens should have significant input and ownership of the time limits that have been set for them.

    Agree   Disagree

11. As I struggle with imposing time limits on my teens, I believe God helps me by:

12. The strength I draw from Psalm 139:11–12 is:

The LORD will keep you from all harm—He
will watch over your life; the LORD will
watch over your coming and going both
now and forevermore. (Psalm 121:7–8)

Not in That Car

A sure sign that our teenagers are maturing is
the first day they go off in a car we are not driving. Whether the new chauffeur is
an older sibling or an older friend of our teens, the experience is unnerving to say
the least. Although it might mean the end of constant chauffeuring on our part,
it also symbolizes a loss of control; no longer can we be assured that once our
teens have gone to the mall, to a party, or to a friend's house, they will remain
there.

While our teens may revel in their new-found freedom, we parents must deal
with fears central to our loss of control: the possibility of serious harm to or even
the death of our teenagers once they are out of our protection. Is it any wonder,
then, that we who are motivated by these fears do what we can to limit our teens'
association with the automobile? These fears lead us to establish limits on our
teenagers' behavior, even though doing so will ultimately lead to more conflict
with them. Although we do have the right—even the obligation—to protect our
teens from all harm and danger, especially when our teens fail to perceive the
possible consequences of their actions, sometimes we let our fears get in the way
of their maturation.

The greatest gift we have as we deal with their freedom and our loss of control
is Christ Himself. Faith in Christ allows us to confess our desire to control the sit-

uations our teens might confront on the road but our powerlessness to do so. The fact that Christ took all sins to the cross allows us to place our worries and fears about our teens at the foot of the cross and commend them to the merciful hands of our almighty God. As we do so, we can take comfort and strength even from the word "good-bye." It comes from an old English word that means, "God be with you." So, as we watch our teens drive away with someone, we can say good-bye and acknowledge that God will indeed "watch over [our teens'] coming and going, both now and forevermore."

Over whose dead body?!?

I'm Maria, and I'm in ninth grade. One day I came home from school earlier than usual and my mom happened to be home. When she asked how I got home, I said that Jill's older brother had picked us up and taken us home.

My mom went ballistic! Jill's older brother is 19 and has had two DWIs in the last three years. In fact, if not for their family lawyer, he wouldn't have been driving at all. My mom told me never to accept a ride with Jill's brother again. I told her that he had learned his lesson and had quit drinking, but she wouldn't listen. All she said was, "I don't care, I don't want you riding in his car!"

"I can accept a ride with anyone I want," I yelled back. "You just don't trust me!"

"Over my dead body you will," she replied. "It's not that I don't trust you; I don't always trust the judgment of people you hang out with. Just one second of poor judgment in any situation and it could be *your* dead body!"

What would you do?

- Finish the conversation between Maria and her mother and resolve their conflict.

- Outline the issues that prevent Maria and her mom from reaching an understanding about acceptable rides for her.

- What would Maria's friend's brother need to do so her mom would be willing to trust his driving ability?

- Maria reflects two common attitudes of teens: nothing will ever happen to me, and I can express my freedom any way I want. As a parent, how would you address both attitudes?

- If parents believe the safety of their teens is at stake, how much can or should they do to assure their teens' safety?

• What other choices does Maria have when confronted with a situation of which her parents disapprove?

It would be great if we could place shields around our teens to protect them from all harm and danger, but we can't. We can, however, eliminate those things that pull us away from the real issue. For instance, many times we let ourselves be sidetracked by unwarranted challenges from our teens that we do not trust them, their judgment, or their friends. Many times we are distracted by our teens' sense of immortality, the sense that leads them to believe "nothing bad will ever happen."

While it may be true that we have difficulty trusting our teens, their judgment, or their friends, we need to be open and honest about our feelings of fear and apprehension. We need to be able to say, "When I am upset, it is often because I am afraid. When I question you, often I am apprehensive. When I say no, it's because I want you to stay alive." Once we are able to admit our fears and bring them out in the open, we can begin a more logical dialogue about our concerns, our opinions, and our ideas.

Even with such a dialogue, we still need to admit—if even just to ourselves—our powerlessness in many situations. No matter what we say, our teens may willingly place themselves in situations where they run the risk of being seriously injured or even killed. As we confess our powerlessness and place ourselves and our children at the foot of the cross, we can look at the seventh petition of the Lord's Prayer in a new way. Each time we pray "deliver us from evil," we can include the names of the people we would ask God to protect—our friends, our teens, ourselves—and trust that His love and protection will never fail.

Closing Prayer

Dear God, You know what it is like to lose a child. As I struggle with the possibility of losing my own son or daughter, calm my fears and relieve my anxieties so I might place my trust in You and You alone, and continue to believe that You will protect me and my family from all harm and danger. For Jesus' sake. Amen

Parent Pairs

What are the 10 most important things you as a parent can do to ensure your teens are, and will remain safe when they are with their friends? What are the 10 most important things your teens can do to ensure their safety? Who are the friends of your teens that cause you the greatest concern about their safety or security? When you pray the petition "deliver us from evil," for whom would you seek God's merciful protection?

Read Psalm 121:7–8 and consider the following questions as you discuss the **Parent Pairs** section with your spouse or another parent.

Not in That Car

(To be done with your spouse or another parent.)

1. The 10 most important things I can do to assure my teens are safe when they are with their friends are: *(Rank these in order of importance, with 1 being the most important and 10 being the least important.)*

   ____ Know exactly where they are and what they will be doing.

   ____ Know the kind of friends my teens will be with.

   ____ Make sure my teens can always use me as an excuse not to do something they consider unsafe, by saying things like, "I'm sorry, blame my parents, don't blame me."

   ____ Make sure my teens are aware of their choices when confronted with situations that may seem dangerous.

   ____ Pray God would keep my teens safe from all harm and danger.

   ____ Participate in organizations that will keep my community and neighborhood safer, such as MADD and neighborhood crime watches.

   ____ Form support networks with parents to set reasonable and safe boundaries for our teenagers.

   ____ Attempt to get to know the parents of my child's friends.

   ____ Be open about my fears and concerns.

   ____ Be clear about my expectations, and consistent and fair about the consequences when those expectations have not been met.

2. The 10 most important things my teens can do to demonstrate they know how to be safe when they are with their friends are: *(Rank these in order of importance, with 1 being the most important and 10 being the least important.)*

   ____ Be open about their fears and concerns.

   ____ Be able to speak for themselves and take a stand even when that stand is not popular or well received.

   ____ Show they listen to me and respect what I say.

97

_____ Have their own sense of boundaries and limits so they can tell what is wrong or what is right, what is healthy and what is harmful.

_____ Demonstrate that what they believe will influence how they act.

_____ Be able to tell me the options they might have and choices they might make when confronted with situations that place them at risk.

_____ Have a sense of their mortality.

_____ Care about the health and welfare of their friends, and the actions their friends may take.

_____ Be able to show that they are dependable and responsible by observing the rules of our household.

_____ Place their own health and welfare above the pleasure and desires of their group.

3. I have shared my concerns with my teens.

        Agree   **Disagree**

4. I like all my teens' friends.

        Agree   **Disagree**

5. Describe the worries or concerns you may have about your teens' friends:

6. When I shared my concerns about their friends with my teens, my sharing helped the situation by:

    It hurt the situation by:

7. If I could voice one concern about my teens' friends, it would be:

8. As I pray the petition, "deliver us from evil," I pray for the protection of the following people:

9. The strength I draw from Psalm 121:7–8 is:

But He said to me, "My grace is sufficient for you, for My power is made perfect in weaknesses." Therefore I will boast all the more gladly about my weaknesses, so that Christ's power may rest in me. (2 Corinthians 12:9)

Just One Drink

Perhaps one of the most frightening experiences for us as parents is the first time our teens are exposed to the availability of drugs or alcohol. It seems to make no difference these days whether we live in a large metropolitan area, a small town, a farming community, or a suburb, drugs and alcohol remain a constant threat to the emotional stability and physical safety of our loved ones.

Faced with the potential of this threat, how do we as parents keep our teens safe from these influences, as well as safe from themselves? The battles of temptation and control are real, and for teens, are made even more complicated by the time of life in which they occur. As children enter adolescence, they desire to grow apart from their families—especially parents—to establish their own identities, test their limits and ours, discover and explore new things, and prove they are growing up. As parents we are torn; on one hand we want to encourage healthy growth, on the other we want to discourage behavior that would be harmful and potentially destructive. If we say too much, we are lecturing; if we say too little, it feels like we're giving our consent to anything our teens wish to do.

As we help our teens deal with the temptation of alcohol and other drugs, we need to remind them of their center in Jesus Christ. We need to help them see how alcoholism and drug addiction can lead them away from Christ and potentially make them slaves to such substances. We need to help our teens recognize that the road to alcohol abuse and addiction is a road that makes them travel away from the true freedom found in Jesus Christ. We need to bring them again and again into God's presence where His grace is revealed through Word and Sacrament and where our teens can be renewed in their faith.

In the midst of our powerlessness, it can be comforting to remember the answer God gave to Paul as he prayed that God would remove a thorn from his flesh: "My grace is sufficient for you, for my power is made perfect in weakness." It is also comforting to read Paul's response: "Therefore I will boast all the more gladly about my weaknesses, so that Christ's power may rest on me." Once again, the answer for us as parents is to rest solely and completely on the grace of God, rejoicing in the comfort that Jesus has overcome the slavery of sin for our sake, as well as the sake of our teens. The tremendous power Jesus conveys—the power of the cross that overcomes abuse and addiction—is available for us and for our teens.

What do you expect me to do?

Rick was a star high school athlete. Already in his junior year, he had been named an all-conference running back for his football team. Expectations ran high for his basketball season as well; there was talk that Rick would not only be an all-conference guard, he also would be named to the all-state team.

The week between football and basketball season, there was a party at Carrie's house to which Rick had been invited. It seemed like everyone from school was there. To make matters a little more exciting, Rick's best friend, Don, had brought along a bottle of vodka. As Rick and Don poured the vodka into their pop cans, no one had any idea that they were drinking until Carrie came up to them and said, "Look guys, my parents will kill me if they find someone has alcohol here. I think you'd better go home!"

Later that evening, around 11:30, Rick and Don were sitting by the garage finishing their last mixed drink, when car headlights blinded them. Rick's parents were pulling up the driveway. Rick's last words to Don were, "O man, I think I'm in big trouble!"

The next morning Rick woke up in his bed, with no idea how he had gotten there. When he came downstairs, the first words from his father were, "Tell me, what do you expect me to do now?"

"About what?" Rick answered.

"About basketball, about privileges like the use of the car, your curfew, what we let you do, all of the above."

What would you do?

- If Rick were your son, what do you think he would say?

- Outline the problems Rick faces. Of those problems, which do you believe is the greatest? What does Rick need to do to solve that problem?

- If you were Rick's father, what would you do about the list already mentioned: basketball, the use of the car, and his curfew?

- What could Rick have done to prevent the situation from occurring?

- What could Rick and his parents have done to prevent the situation from occurring?

- What rules could Rick's parents have developed that might have helped Rick resist taking the first drink, then continuing to drink throughout the evening?

- If you were Rick's parents, would you talk to Don or Don's parents? If you chose to talk with them, what would you say?

Perhaps the most harmful attitude any parent can take is "teens will be teens," or "thank God my teens only drank beer, and no other drugs were involved." Even at this age, teens need parents to set limits for them. As discussed in chapter 10, setting limits responsibly and within reason is a sign of a parent who loves his or her teens. It's also important to consider that studies done by chemical dependency experts have shown that the stronger parents voice their opposition to teen drinking, and the stiffer the consequences for those who drink, the later in life that teens will decide to begin experimenting with drugs or alcohol.

Parents who have experienced their sons or daughters coming home after a night of being under the influence of drugs or alcohol can remember the pain, anxiety, fear, and countless other feelings associated with teen usage of drugs and alcohol. If parents have not shared that experience with their teens, they should know it's only by the grace of God that they haven't—yet. All parents can take comfort knowing that same grace, the undeserved love of Christ, is sufficient for us, as well as our teens. Even in the midst of temptation and weakness, God's strength, as revealed in His Word and received through the body and blood of Christ, will prevail, giving us the comfort, hope, and above all, the courage to live out our faith in and love for Christ Jesus.

Closing Prayer

O God, all too often I feel helpless about my ability to influence my teens' choices, and powerless to protect them from choices that may lead to harm. When I am overwhelmed and preoccupied by the dangers of the world and the potential of those dangers to affect my teens, strengthen me with Your grace. Finally, Lord, help me to see that Your strength is made complete in my weakness, and Your grace is sufficient for me. In Jesus' name. Amen.

Parent Pairs

What concerns do you have about the potential for your teens to use alcohol or other drugs? How clearly have you communicated to your teens the consequences that would result from their use of alcohol or other drugs? What do you need from your church or from your teens' school to help you deal with issues of alcohol and drug use? How can God help you as you deal with these concerns?

Read 2 Corinthians 12:9 and consider the following questions as you discuss the **Parent Pairs** section with your spouse or another parent.

Just One Drink

(To be done with your spouse or another parent.)

1. I have concerns about my teens' use of alcohol or drugs.

   Agree   Disagree

2. My teens know what I will do if I discover they have drunk alcohol or used drugs.

   Agree   Disagree

3. I have concerns about my teens' friends' use of alcohol or drugs.

   Agree   Disagree

4. If I caught my teens drinking with their friends, I would talk to their friends' parents.

   Agree   Disagree

5. I think it's only a part of becoming a man or a woman to experiment with drugs and alcohol.

   Agree   Disagree

6. People have voiced concerns about my own use of drugs or alcohol.

   Agree   Disagree

7. In the past, when I have caught my son or daughter with drugs or alcohol, I have:

8. My reaction helped the situation by:

9. My reaction harmed the situation by:

10. If I could change one thing about the way I react or have reacted to my teens' use or potential use of alcohol, it would be:

11. If I could say one thing to those parents who struggle with their teens' drug or alcohol use, it would be:

12. I realize I need support from various places and people as I try to deal with my teens' use or potential use of alcohol and drugs.

From the school I can receive:

From the church I can receive:

From the parents of my teens' friends I can receive:

From my community I can receive:

From my spouse or significant other I can receive:

From my teens I can receive:

From the courts and legal system I can receive:

From God I can receive:

13. God can help me deal with issues about drugs and alcohol by:

14. The strength I draw from 2 Corinthians 12:9 is:

And Jesus grew in wisdom and stature, and
in favor with God and men.
(Luke 2:52)

Behind the Wheel

One of the greatest events in a teen's life is the
day they get their driver's license. Some call the process one of the only true rites
of passage left in American culture; teens might agree. Here at last is proof of
their independence, proof of their maturation. They now have license to go any-
where they choose—assuming, of course, they have a car and their parents' permission.

One of the scariest events in parents' lives is the day their teens get their driver's licenses. As hard as it was for parents to let their teens merely get into a car
another teen was driving, it's 10 times worse now that their teens are the ones
doing the driving. Many of the same feelings arise as their teens hit the roads: a
loss of control, a sense of sadness at the realization that their teens are no longer
children, an intense fear for the safety and well-being of their teens—and other
drivers. Of course, we as parents want our teenagers to be confident, safe drivers.
But how will they get there, if even we are afraid to step into a car with them?

It might take a long time before the word "safe" applies to our offspring. As we
go from one crisis to another, it is important for us to remember that Jesus also
experienced the perils of growing as a teen in His society. The Luke text states
Jesus "grew in wisdom and stature, and in favor with God and men." Reading
between the lines, however, we wonder what events Jesus and His earthly parents

might have experienced as Jesus grew in wisdom and in stature.

Luke's commentary on Jesus' growth comes immediately after Mary and Joseph leave Jerusalem without 12-year-old Jesus. When a very upset Mary finally finds Him in the temple, she states what every mother or father have at one time or another said to their teenager, "Son, why have You treated us like this?" As we experience our struggles and our anxieties with our teens—especially about driving a car—God experiences these struggles with us. In fact, God helps us realize that even in the midst of our teens' driving experience, they too will continue to grow in wisdom and stature and in favor with God and people.

But it was green!

Laney had gotten her driver's permit three months earlier, after passing her written test. Periodically her father, Jim, would let her drive as he ran various errands for the family. One Sunday evening, Jim figured it would be a good time for Laney to practice by driving to the store to drop off a video due that evening.

As usual, Jim's plan was to take the long way to the store so she would have more time to practice driving. Included in the route was time spent on the freeway, as well as several right- and left-hand turns on busy streets. Jim prided himself on staying calm and not commenting much on Laney's driving—his way of trying to build his daughter's confidence and making the drive a pleasurable, rewarding experience.

Trouble came, however, when after they dropped off the video, Laney signaled to get into the left turn lane. She made the lane switch successfully and approached the intersection. The light was green, but since she was turning, she had to yield to oncoming cars. Jim was prepared for Laney to put on the brake and wait for the cars to pass before she would turn left, but before Jim knew it, Laney was turning into the path of an oncoming truck.

"No!" Jim screamed. Amazingly, the truck swerved, Laney put her foot on the gas, and they made it through the intersection unscathed.

"Pull over," Jim said.

They pulled over to the curb. While Jim figured out what to do next, Laney said, "The light was green in my lane, so I thought I could go!"

What would you do?

> • Finish the conversation between Laney and Jim. If you were Jim, what would you do next?

- What other information about the situation would be helpful to have before you make any conclusions?

- Jim thought the best course of action was to say little, if anything, to Laney about her driving. If you were Jim, what style of instruction would you have adopted to teach Laney to drive?

- Before Laney goes out to drive again, what does she need to do?

- Before Jim invites Laney to drive with him again, what does Jim need to do?

- If Jim's goal as a dad is to help build Laney's confidence as a driver, what might be the best way for him to accomplish his goal?

Parents may consider themselves fully equipped with all the teaching skills in the world, and still have their entire perspective change when they step into a car with their teen behind the wheel. Obviously our greatest immediate concerns as we drive with our teens are for their safety, our safety, and the safety of other people who might ride with them or cross their vehicle's path. Short of never allowing them to drive a vehicle, the most we can do as parents when driving with our teens is not to shrink away from our teaching responsibilities. They need us, as well as our experience, to reassure them that when they drive, they and everyone else will be safe. At the same time, we need to make their safety our first priority by not putting them in dangerous situations and by constantly warning them of dangers that may lie ahead. We hope any conflict that might come as a result of our verbal coaching is taken as a normal part of the learning process.

Behind our fear is also the recognition that the beginning of our teens' driving experience is a significant milestone in our lives too. It takes them one step closer to the time when they will leave our homes and be on their own. Obtaining a driver's license is a definite sign our teens are increasing in wisdom and stature. As we engage in the steps that lead to their driving—and thus maturation—it is important for us as parents to recognize that their driving symbolizes a loss for us: we are closer to the time when they will no longer be under our control. With that in mind, it is even more important to come into His presence to be embraced by His grace through Word and Sacrament and to bring our feelings to the throne of God our Heavenly Father. As we do, we trust that He will continue to love us and care for us even as we acknowledge our loss.

Closing Prayer

O gracious God, life passes so quickly for me and my teens as they grow in years and in wisdom. As I see my teens change and begin to learn to drive, I pray You will keep them from all harm and danger. I pray also that You would give me strength, patience, and perseverance to trust that when my teens drive, You drive with them as well. Into Your hands I commend them, O God. In Jesus' name. Amen.

Parent Pairs

If you were to rank the 10 most important concerns about your teens' driving, what would that ranking look like? What would be your most important concern? Your least important concern? How comfortable are you with your teens' driving ability? Are your teens risk-takers behind the wheel or are they safety-conscious? As you and your teens experience this significant milestone, what might your prayer be for both you and them?

Read Luke 2:52 and consider the following questions as you discuss the **Parent Pairs** section with your spouse or another parent.

Behind the Wheel

(To be done with your spouse or another parent.)

1. As my teens learn to drive, the 10 most important characteristics they need to possess before I will feel comfortable about their ability to drive safely are: *(Rank these in order of importance, with 1 being the most important and 10 being the least important.)*

   _____ They know and obey all traffic laws.

   _____ They show they can drive defensively.

   _____ They understand driving is a privilege and not a right.

   _____ They are able to pay for their own insurance and gas.

   _____ They are willing to take the car only when I let them.

   _____ They are financially stable enough to buy their own car.

   _____ They feel comfortable about operating the car in every possible situation.

   _____ They show me they will come home when they say they will, and go only where they say they will go.

   _____ They say no to drinking and driving.

   _____ They know and accept my consequences for when they do not meet my expectations.

2. I feel comfortable and confident about my teens' driving ability.

   Agree   Disagree

3. My teens have shown me they will not take any risks when it comes to operating an automobile.

   Agree   Disagree

4. My teens and I have established consequences for violating my expectations.

   Agree   Disagree

5. If I were to advise other parents who were going to begin the driver's training process with their teens, I would say:

6. If I could give one piece of advice that I have learned about driving to other parents of teens it would be:

7. If my teens fail to get good grades, they are not allowed to drive.

   Agree   Disagree

8. If I could change two things about the way my teens drive or want to drive, they would be:

9. If I could change two things about the way I react to my teens' driving, they would be:

10. When it comes to teen driving, I wish our driver's education programs would: *(You may choose more than one answer.)*
    ❏ Help our teens take driving more seriously.
    ❏ Do a more thorough job of educating young drivers.
    ❏ Have classes for parents on how to relate to their teens who are learning how to drive.
    ❏ Do nothing more than they already do.

11. When it comes to teen driving, I wish our state would: *(You may choose more than one answer.)*

❑ Make each teen wait until they are 18 before allowing them to drive.

❑ Expand the length of drivers' training programs so the instruction is more thorough and teens would have more skills before they earn their license.

❑ Subsidize the cost of drivers' training programs so they are more affordable to everyone.

❑ I'm perfectly satisfied with the way things are.

12. My prayer for my teens as they begin to drive is:

13. My prayer for myself as my teens begin to drive is:

14. The strength I draw from Luke 2:52 is:

And now these three remain: faith, hope
and love. But the greatest of these is love.
(1 Corinthians 13:13)

Love and ...

Just when we think our sons and daughters are
old enough to make responsible and rational decisions, they come home one day
with a glassy-eyed look. It's not that they're drunk; it's that they've finally found
the "one they love." Their discovery can not only turn their lives upside down, it
can turn their families upside down as well.

Space has to be made to give teens room to explore their new relationships.
Places need to be set aside for teens to "hang out" in the safety and privacy of
their home. Families need time to get used to the idea, as well as adjust to the
change in personality of the teens who are experiencing their new-found love.
Parents need to be aware that as their teens go through this new emotional
adjustment, they are discovering who they are in relationship to other people.
During this period of discovery, identities and behavior may change drastically.

How much change is beneficial? How can teens fall in love without being swal-
lowed up by the idea of romantic love? As parents and teens face this important
time in their lives, we as parents can do our teens a favor by helping them understand what Paul says in 1 Corinthians 13, sometimes known as the "great love
chapter" of the Bible. The love Paul describes is agape love, love that is grace-
centered. This love is much more than "being" in love or "falling" in love. Agape
means that two people love each other the way God loves them—totally and

unconditionally, without any strings attached, warts and all.

In the midst of the uncertainty and change as our teens search for the meaning of love and the one they love, the God who said it was not good for man and woman to be alone is the God who blesses our teens as they discover the joy of being together. He will continue to help both us parents and our teens discover the joy of agape love, and empower us all to reflect that same love in our relationships with one another. He will empower our teens to seek agape love in their own relationships, so that as they grow to love one another, they will begin to know more about the God who loves them totally and unconditionally, warts and all.

Trapped by love ...

Jenny's mom, Tina, was straightening up Jenny's desk. When she moved Jenny's library book, a piece of paper fell out. Tina's mouth dropped open as she read the following letter:

Dear Teen Advisor:

I'm 15 and I've been dating this 16-year-old guy for the last six months. At first my parents were against it, but now they think he's a pretty cool guy and especially my dad doesn't mind having him around.

My problem is that a month ago, he told me he loved me. When he said it, I couldn't believe it. I was happier than I had ever been before. I never thought anybody like Steve would even date me, much less love me. But now, a month later, things seem to have changed. I'm not even talking about the physical side of our relationship, although that's changed too.

Steve claims that if we really love each other, we would want to spend as much time as we can together. At first I thought the idea was great. But now, it's like I never see my friends any more. I used to have one night a week for my friends, and one night on the weekend for Steve; now it has to be all Steve. I feel suffocated. I feel trapped. I feel like if this is love, who needs it?

I told all that to Steve, but he just said, "I thought you loved me!"

I love Steve, but I want to see my friends. What should I do?

Signed,
Trapped by Love

Tina put down the letter and called her husband. When he got on the phone she said, "Rick, we need to talk about Jenny and Steve!"

What would you do?

- If you were Jenny's mom, under what circumstances would you, or would you not, have read Jenny's letter to the teen advisor?
- What options do Rick and Tina have as they consider what they will do about Jenny and Steve?
- Pretend you are Rick and Tina and you approach Jenny. What will you say?
- What do you believe Jenny needs from her parents right now?
- Jenny says the physical side of her relationship with Steve has changed. How might Rick and Tina approach that concern as well?
- Pretend you are the teen advisor to whom the letter is addressed. Write a response to Jenny who is "trapped by love."

Parents walk a fine line when it comes to communicating their concerns about the relationships their teens have with the opposite sex. The concerns become exceedingly difficult to express, especially when one or both parents have reservations about how the relationship might change the behavior and relationships their teens have with other friends.

As we find ourselves in this situation, remember we have the right to voice our concerns. To be the most effective, address the situation in a way that in no way cuts down the significant other of your teens. Focusing on the significant other may serve only to drive us farther apart than we already may be.

Instead, we can focus on our teens by saying things like, "Jenny, you never seem to have time for your friends any more. How do you feel about that? How do they feel about that?" We can also focus on the change in their behavior. "Jenny, you used to love to swim, play tennis, and jog. Now it seems like you're always too tired to do any of the things you used to like. Do you miss those things? Would you like to do them again?" Or, "Jenny, you used to be a straight-A student who loved school. Now you hate school and your grades have dropped. What's going on?" By focusing on our teens' behavior, we help them become more accountable for themselves. We empower them to be more responsible for their own actions. We give them permission to be who they want to be—perhaps who they once were.

Remember that God loves us totally, completely, and unconditionally with agape love through the gift of His Son Jesus Christ, who died on the cross for our sins and rose again so we might be with Him forever. Empowered by His love, God will give us the strength to love our teenagers totally and unconditionally as well, reflecting the same love and forgiveness God continues to shower on us all.

Closing Prayer

O God, You created the first man and woman to love each other. So too You have given my teens the gift of relationships. Help them even as they celebrate the gift of their relationships to continue to come to You with their concerns, and to continue to depend upon You as the source of their identity and the fountain of their strength. In Jesus' name. Amen.

Parent Pairs

What are the most important characteristics you believe the people who date your teens should possess? How do you believe your teens would answer that same question? What would you do if your teens' dating relationships changed their pattern of behavior or circle of friends? How can understanding God's love help you deal with your teens as they experience the joys and sorrows of romantic love?

Read 1 Corinthians 13:13 and consider the following questions as you discuss the **Parent Pairs** section with your spouse or another parent.

Love and ...

(To be done with your spouse or another parent.)

1. I believe the people my teens date need to:

Agree	Disagree	Be completely trustworthy.
Agree	Disagree	Come from the same type of family background and values.
Agree	Disagree	Come from the same religious background.
Agree	Disagree	Be liked by my teens.
Agree	Disagree	Have goals for their lives.
Agree	Disagree	Be as intelligent as my teens.
Agree	Disagree	Bring out the best in my teens.
Agree	Disagree	Have the same interests as my teens.
Agree	Disagree	Be mature and act responsibly.
Agree	Disagree	Treat my teens with respect.

2. Following are three characteristics I believe are the most important characteristics of those who date my teens.

   a.

   b.

   c.

3. Following are three characteristics I believe are the least important characteristics of those who date my teens.

   a.

   b.

   c.

4. If my teens described the three most important characteristics of their dates, they would be:

a.

b.

c.

5. If my teens described the three least important characteristics of their dates, they would be:

a.

b.

c.

6. If my teens' relationships with significant others change their behavior, grades, relationships with other friends, I would: *(You may choose more than one answer.)*

☐ Do nothing. It would be their problem.

☐ Tell them my fears.

☐ Describe the changes I saw, and ask them what they wanted to do about those changes.

☐ Forbid them to see their significant other.

7. Understanding God's love helps me deal with my teens as they experience the joys and sorrows of teen love by:

8. The strength I draw from 1 Corinthians 13:13 is:

For this reason a man will leave his father
and mother and be united to his wife,
and they will become one flesh.
(Genesis 2:24)

It's a Three-Letter Word

As liberated and contemporary as our society might be, we often hesitate to be open about sex. In fact, many parents still hold that "the less we know about our children's sexual activity, and the less we talk about sex in the house, the better off we all will be." As a result, sex education has been taken out of the home and put into the classroom. Usually in fifth grade, "the film" is seen, more often than not with boys and girls in separate rooms to minimize the natural embarrassed giggle effect that usually accompanies the film. Around eighth grade, another course about sex is taught, warning students about the dangers of promiscuity as well as the perils of sexually transmitted diseases.

The question the church and we as parents need to address is: As we teach facts and needed information about sexual activity, are we simultaneously teaching about the virtues of fidelity and chastity, as well as the joy and trust of experiencing sex within the marriage relationship? Many instructors may use words like "committed relationships" and "lifelong partner," without asking students what those relationships might look like or without saying anything about the marriage relationship. What's a parent to do?

In the face of the values and mindset society conveys, we as parents need not be powerless; we need only reclaim our biblical heritage. The creation story explains the marriage relationship and places sex within its proper context. From the perspective of the garden, sex is not a casual experience; it reflects the ultimate in communication between Adam and Eve. As they communicate their love for each other in this way, they reflect a permanent commitment blessed by God. Within the context of that commitment, they felt no shame.

Isn't that same sense of commitment, blessed by God, what we want for our teens? Don't we want them to experience sex from within the context of a marriage? As parents, we need not be afraid to reflect those values to our teens and convey to them a sense of a responsible God who intentionally created them with the gift of their sexuality, a gift He intended for them to use within the bonds of marriage. From that context, freed from guilt and shame, they will be able to enjoy their sexual relationships with so much more joy.

My lifelong partner

Barry and Audrey's daughter, Amy, was in eighth grade at Bolivar Middle School. One evening at the dinner table, Audrey began the conversation by asking, "What did you talk about in school today, Amy?"

"We talked about pre-marital sex," Amy said.

Amy's response made Barry and Audrey immediately uncomfortable. Both Barry and Audrey had come from a strict background. Both were raised by parents who communicated the silent message, "the less said about sex the better!" Although they had grown up in a period where the mores and values of the country had been widening, they were still uncomfortable even mentioning the word sex in front of one another, let alone their daughter.

Barry took a deep breath and asked, "What did your teacher say about sex?"

"Mrs. Diego told us that sex should be reserved for our lifelong partner!"

Barry and Audrey looked at each other in wide-eyed amazement. Audrey thought, "The nerve of a teacher trying to define when the appropriate time is for my daughter to have sex. Besides, I knew plenty of boys in high school who would have been glad to say they wanted to be my lifelong partner."

Audrey looked at Amy and asked, "Amy, how will you know when your lifelong partner comes along?"

What would you do?

• If you were Barry and Audrey, what information would you want to know from Amy's teacher, Mrs. Diego, before proceeding with any reaction to Amy's statement?

- Assuming you had the information from Mrs. Diego, what more would you say to Amy?

- What if Amy were to reply, "Mom, Dad, how will I know when I want to spend the rest of my life with someone?" How would you, as Amy's parents, reply?

- Analyze Mrs. Diego's statement. What makes her statement about sex being reserved for one's lifelong partner a helpful statement for Amy?

- From the other point of view, what makes Mrs. Diego's statement about sex being reserved for one's lifelong partner a harmful statement for Amy?

- If you were the pastor of Barry and Audrey and they came to you with this subject, how would you react? What would you say to Amy about what the church believes?

As much as we might try to avoid the topic of sex with our teens, they still need a sense of limits and boundaries in their relationships and need our help in setting them. The temptation for parents is to dramatize any situation involving sex, and through the dramatization, make it out to be much worse than it actually is. But we needn't be afraid to communicate our fears to our teens, fears that are the result of actual histories. Yes Amy, we might say, people actually do die from AIDS. Yes Amy, when you are 18, you may believe you have found your lifelong partner, but your ideal lifelong partner at 18 may not be the person you would want at 28.

We need to be willing to listen to and be open to our teens' concerns without sacrificing our own beliefs about what is right and wrong. We need to help our teens set limits, and help them recognize that lifelong relationships are not always easy to discern at their start. Finally, we need to communicate to our teens the value of committed married sex, and the freedom as well as the joy God intended committed married sex to bring to both partners. Above all, remember God is faithful to us and our teenagers as we struggle with the issues of sex, love, and intimacy. He accepts us as we struggle, and loves us with a love that will never end.

Closing Prayer

Lord God, You created us as sexual human beings. Help me support my teens as they struggle to use their sexuality in a responsible, faithful manner that protects and preserves their integrity and individuality, and ultimately gives glory to You. In Jesus' name. Amen.

Parent Pairs

If you found out your teens were having sex with their partners, what would you do, how would you react? If you found out your teens and their partners were pregnant, what would you do, how would you react? Have you taken the time to communicate the value of waiting until marriage to have sex, as well as the advantages of committed married sex, to your teens?

Read Genesis 2:24 and consider the following questions as you discuss the **Parent Pairs** section with your spouse or another parent.

It's a Three-Letter Word

(To be done with your spouse or another parent.)

1. If I found out my teens were having sex, I would: *(You may choose more than one answer.)*
   - ❏ Call the partners' parents and have a meeting.
   - ❏ Talk to my teens and find out more about their feelings for the other people.
   - ❏ Hit the roof, the walls, the ceiling, and any other inanimate object within my reach.
   - ❏ Blame myself for having failed my teens in some way.

2. If I found out my teens were having sex, I would: *(You may choose more than one answer.)*
   - ❏ Make sure they were using responsible birth control.
   - ❏ Warn them against the dangers of sexually transmitted diseases.
   - ❏ Make my teens go to a different school, perhaps move to a different state.
   - ❏ Do nothing, because it was bound to happen sooner or later.

3. If I discovered that my daughter was pregnant, I would: *(You may choose more than one answer.)*
   - ❏ Make her give the baby up for adoption.
   - ❏ Arrange for her to marry the father.
   - ❏ Tell her I will do nothing to help her with the child, especially financially.
   - ❏ Welcome her with open arms and anxiously await the birth of my grandchild.
   - ❏ See what other arrangements could be made.

4. If I discovered that my son was about to be a father, I would: *(You may choose more than one answer.)*
   - ❏ Insist he make the mother give the baby up for adoption.

❏ Arrange for him to marry the mother.

❏ Remind him of his financial responsibility and tell him that I will do nothing to help the child financially.

❏ Welcome him with open arms and anxiously await the birth of my grandchild.

❏ See what other arrangements could be made.

5. My greatest fear about my teens having sex before marriage is: *(You may choose more than one answer.)*

❏ A pregnancy might result.

❏ They might contract a sexually transmitted disease.

❏ They would be robbed of their childhood.

❏ I would be stuck raising their child.

6. What I believe my teens need from the church to help them deal with the issue of sexual activity is: *(You may choose more than one answer.)*

❏ Acceptance and understanding that it is a difficult and tempting world out there.

❏ A stronger voice preaching against sex before marriage.

❏ More emphasis on chastity and fidelity in relationships.

❏ More opportunity for healthy relationship building, like church activities for my teens and their dates.

7. Two things I would need from the church if I discovered my teens were having sex would be:

8. Two things I would need from my friends if I discovered my teens were having sex would be:

9. Two things I would need from my teens if I discovered they were having sex would be:

10. If I were to communicate to my teens the advantages of waiting until marriage to have sex, I would say:

11. The strength I draw from Genesis 2:24 is:

On the third day a wedding took place
at Cana in Galilee. Jesus' mother was there,
and Jesus and His disciples had also been
invited to the wedding. (John 2:1–2)

The Date's Been Set

When the announcement is made, it would
seem the parents' roles are complete. They have raised their children to adulthood and the pinnacle is reached as each proclaims, "I'm getting married!" Joy
and jubilation should abound; the parents' jobs are done; the teens are moving on.
But many aspects of this announcement can be problematic to say the least.

No matter how parents look at it, engagement and marriage bring the potential of loss. Relationships will never be the same again. If grief isn't the order of
the day, then perhaps finances are. There's no getting around it: weddings are
expensive. Even more costly, perhaps, is the hassle of planning and carrying out
a wedding. Many parents have offered their son or daughter the equivalent in
cash of what a wedding would cost, if only the son or daughter would quietly
elope. A great deal of consternation and friction may also arise when it is per-
ceived the darling daughter or strapping son is too young or has become engaged
to someone the parents consider to be "the wrong person."

No matter how we feel, nothing makes us more aware that our children ultimately do not belong to us than their decision to be married. As we think about
the event, it might be good for us to remember the ideal marriage conveyed in
Scripture is not between a man and a woman, but between Christ and His
church. Paul, in his letter to the Ephesians, says "Husbands, love your wives, just

as Christ loved the church and gave Himself up for her" (Ephesians 5:25).

In many respects then, it is no surprise that Jesus' first miracle takes place at the wedding of Cana in Galilee. His presence there was a blessing upon that marriage; His changing water into wine became a commentary on how Christ, as the bridegroom, treats His church, the bride. In love, Christ gave up His life for the church so we might be freed from the power of sin and death and have eternal life with Him in heaven. As we look forward to the day when our teens get married, may we pray that the love they share with their prospective husbands or wives might reflect that love God has given them through their Lord and Savior Jesus Christ.

Susie, you're way too young!

Susie had dated Craig for the past two years. The day of her high school graduation had arrived and Craig, a sophomore in college, had come home for the graduation. The night before commencement exercises, Craig and Susie walked into Susie's parents living room and joyously announced to her mom and dad, "We're getting married!"

Bill, Susie's dad, asked, "Well, uh, what date did you have in mind?"

Craig replied, "Next June, after my junior year. That will mean I'll have only one year left, and I'll have taken all my core requirements by then. We figure the money we save this coming year will help us make it through any tough financial times during our first year of marriage."

Carol, Susie's mom, had never been that fond of Craig, although she wasn't sure why. But she was also worried that they were getting married way too young. Slowly Carol asked, "Susie, what about college?"

Susie replied, "Mom, that's no big deal! I can go to college any time I want. Besides, I think it's a waste of time to go right now, especially since I have no idea what I would go to school for!"

Fighting back the tears, Carol finally blurted out, "Susie, you're just too young!" Then she stomped out of the room.

Bill just stared into space and said nothing.

What would you do?

• If you were Bill or Carol, how would you have initially reacted to the announcement of Craig and Susie's engagement?

- What might Bill and Carol have done to have been better prepared for Susie and Craig's "joyous" announcement?

- Besides Carol's pointing out that Susie is too young, if you were Carol, or Bill for that matter, what other concerns would you want to express?

- Bill says absolutely nothing after Carol leaves. If you were Bill, what more would you say? What would make you stay in the room with Craig and Susie? What would make you follow Carol out of the room?

- What can Craig and Susie do to turn the situation into one in which everyone wins?

- If you were Bill and Carol, after the initial shock, what would you decide to do? What would you want to say to Susie, to Craig?

Marriage is a wonderful institution, a blessing from God to both children and parents. Sometimes, though, the announcement of the impending marriage does not strike chords of joy in the hearts of anxious parents. When the announcement seems mistimed, when—in the eyes of parents—the couple seems to be mismatched or too young, parents need the wisdom of Solomon to hold their feelings in check, and still be as supportive as possible for their children.

No matter when the time comes, we as parents need to pray for our children, as well as their future mates. We need not be afraid to ask God to guide our teens as they select their future husbands and wives. For as Jesus gladdened the wedding at Cana in Galilee, so too will He bring joy to the weddings of our children.

Praying for our children allows us to be there for them, listen to their concerns, and keep any negative opinions we may have about the relationship or our future in-laws in a proper perspective. Although our guidance is still necessary, many times the best way to serve our children is by simply being there, especially if the marriage or relationship turns out to be harmful or does not survive. Then, if the worst possible scenario becomes a reality, if we have kept our criticism to ourselves, we will be able to support our children and help them pick up the pieces of their broken lives. Ultimately our support of them will mirror God's faithfulness to us and all His children. For even in the midst of broken earthly relationships, God's relationship with His people never ends.

Closing Prayer

Lord Jesus, You were present at the wedding at Cana, and You blessed it with Your love. In the same way, be present in the marriage of my child. Bless their marriage, so by Your love they might be a blessing to one another and to all. Amen.

Parent Pairs

When is the right time for your teens to be married? What are the important characteristics your teens' prospective mates need to possess? How important is it that your teens participate in paying for at least some of their wedding? How might you best support your teens as they look forward to the day of their wedding and their new married life? If you pray for the prospective mates of your teens, what do you pray for?

Read John 2:1–2 and consider the following questions as you discuss the **Parent Pairs** section with your spouse or another parent.

The Date's Been Set

(To be done with your spouse or another parent.)

1. I believe the right age for my teens to be married is: _____.

2. When my teens get married I hope:
   a. Education-wise they will be:

   b. Financially they will be:

   c. Career-wise they will be:

   d. Education-wise their partners will be:

   e. Financially their partners will be:

   f. Career-wise their partners will be:

3. If my teens got married within the first year after high school, I would:
   a. Help pay for the wedding.

   b. Not pay a dime for anything having to do with the wedding.

4. I believe the people my teens marry need to:

Agree	Disagree	Be completely trustworthy.
Agree	Disagree	Be from the same type of family background and values.
Agree	Disagree	Have the same religious background.
Agree	Disagree	Be liked by my teens.
Agree	Disagree	Have goals for their lives.
Agree	Disagree	Be as intelligent as my teens.
Agree	Disagree	Bring out the best in my teens.
Agree	Disagree	Have the same interests as my teens.

Agree   Disagree   Be mature and act responsibly.

Agree   Disagree   Treat my teens with respect.

5. Three characteristics I believe are the most important in the people who marry my teens are:

a.

b.

c.

6. Three characteristics I believe are the least important in the people who marry my teens are:

a.

b.

c.

7. If I could give my teens one piece of advice about getting married, I would say:

8. I could best support my teens' marriages, by:

9. As I anticipate the day when my teens might be married, my prayer for their future spouses is:

10. The strength I draw from John 2:1–2 is:

The LORD had said to Abram,
"Leave your country, your people
and your father's household
and go to the land I will show you."
(Genesis 12:1)

No One Wants to Leave

In today's world, it is perfectly normal for people to change careers, to buy and sell houses, to move into new neighborhoods and new communities more than once in a lifetime. In the midst of the decision-making though, it's easy to forget that changing careers, homes, and communities for parents, means changing schools and friends for teens. The suggestion of a move may result in high resistance from teens who are attached to friends, teachers, and schools.

As we consider moves that in the long term may benefit our families, but in the short term cause what teens consider permanent damage, we need to be sensitive to the grieving process at work within our families. Moving means loss, and loss leads to grief. Problems for us parents occur when we become so involved in the newness of the situation, we fail to recognize the dynamics of grief our teens are experiencing. What seems to be so self-evident to parents—life will go on—may be impossible for teens to see. Their world has fallen apart, and it can be very difficult to see how the shattered pieces will ever come together again.

Many years ago, God called Abram and Sarai to move from their home in Haran to the land of Canaan. Abram moved because of his faith in God's promises to bless him, make him a great nation, make his name great, and through him, bless all the nations of the earth. God's presence gave Abram the courage to move, leave everything he knew behind, and experience great changes for himself and his relatives.

As we deal with the process of change in our families, we as parents need to remember that no matter how many changes we make, God never changes. God is our source of strength, whether we change or remain the same. He communicates His strength through His written Word and reveals His strength through the Word made flesh—Christ Himself. In turn, we can be sensitive to the needs of our teens, and be confident that if we do move, the God who blessed Abram will continue to bless, guide, and protect us and our families.

I'm not going!

My name is Sam. I'm 42 and the father of two children: Jacki, 14, and Nick, a senior in high school. I just got a promotion to a middle-management position at the home office. We've lived in this small town for 15 years. Jacki was born here; Nick was only 3 when we came. So no one wants to move. Let Jacki tell you her side of the story.

I'm Jacki. All my life I have lived in a town of 2500 people. My dad just got word that he's been transferred to another job in a large city some 500 miles away from here. None of us wants to go. My mom hates the idea. She's established a good life here. She loves our community and she's convinced that where we live is the best place to raise Nick and me. I don't want to leave my friends. My brother Nick is a high school senior, and he's been going with the same girl for three years. He really doesn't want to move.

My dad? He claims he's doing what God wants him to do. I wonder how he can be so convinced of what God wants, especially when he knows how all of us have reacted to the possibility of moving. What about us? What does God want for us? And what does God want us to do, be unhappy?

What would you do?

- According to Jacki, her dad, Sam, says he's doing what God wants. What does this mean?

- Jacki asks the question: "What does God want us to do, be unhappy?" How might God be involved in this process for the family?

- What are the important issues for Sam to recognize? About his family? About his career?

- How should Sam respond to Jacki's concerns?

- What might Jacki do to deal with her grief?

- What more information do you need to help resolve this conflict?

- If you were Sam, what would you do now?

Moves can be inevitable, but as we parents contemplate them, we need to take into consideration the emotional wants and needs of our teenagers. When the possibilities of a move arise, as parents we need to come to the touch point of His presence in worship and devote our time in prayer. Fed by the means of grace, we pray that we might make a God-pleasing choice that takes into consideration all variables—even our teens.

We need to remember this is a grieving situation for all involved. We can't expect everyone to be happy when members of the family are experiencing their own sense of loss. As a result, we need to let the grieving happen, accepting the feelings of anger, sadness, depression, and protest as they happen. The less personally we take these feelings, the better off we will be in supporting our teens.

New friendships for our teens may not be established quickly or easily. It is important for them during this time of transition to maintain contact with old friends. If at all possible, we need to give permission to the different ways our teens may wish to stay in contact with their friends, especially if the move is within a day's drive. This may mean we spend a great amount of weekend time driving back and forth between our new home and our former place of residence, but the time will be well spent.

As we become involved in our new place of work or new home, it can be easy for us as adults to become absorbed in meeting the demands of the new situation and to place those demands above the needs of our family members. Therefore, it will be beneficial for us to create specific family time. Visit neighborhood parks as a family. Explore, discover, and enjoy what the new community has to offer for all the family members. Together make decisions about which organizations to join.

In all, we can continue to trust that God knows all about change. He gave His Son, Jesus Christ, to suffer and die for the sins of humankind, so we might be changed from sinners to saints, from no people to God's people. But even in the midst of this change and all others, our God and His love for us remains the same.

Closing Prayer

O God, all too often things change in my life. When those changes occur, members of my family become threatened because of the losses they experience, and their fear of the unknown future. As we face those changes, help us remember that You never change. Your love and care for us remains the same, not only now, but always. In Your Son's precious name. Amen.

Parent Pairs

How often has your family moved? How have your teens reacted to each move? What made a move successful? What made a move painful? As you review the moves you and your family have already experienced, how might you make your next move different to help your family adjust more easily to the prospects of leaving friends and home behind? How do you know your move might be pleasing to God?

Read Genesis 12:1 and consider the following questions as you discuss the **Parent Pairs** section with your spouse or another parent.

No One Wants to Leave

(To be done with your spouse or another parent.)

1. Our family has moved:
   - ❑ Once in the last five years.
   - ❑ Twice in the last five years.
   - ❑ More than twice in the last 10 years.
   - ❑ We've never moved.

2. Each time our family has moved:
   - ❑ The move was welcomed by everyone.
   - ❑ It was a split decision; some wanted to move, some didn't.
   - ❑ Moves for us have never been easy.
   - ❑ It almost caused our family to break apart.

3. The one time we moved and everything went smoothly was:

4. Three reasons it went smoothly were:

5. The one time we moved and everything went poorly was:

6. Three reasons why it went poorly were:

7. Three things I have learned about making a move and how it affects my family are:

8. Before we make our next move, I need to consider: *(Rank these in order of importance, with 1 being the most important and 10 being the least important.)*

_____ The amount of money I will receive from my job transfer.

_____ The age of my children and how they will be affected by the move.

_____ The kind of community to which we will move.

_____ The number and the quality of schools.

_____ The distance the new home might be from our previous residence.

_____ The availability of work for my spouse.

_____ The length we have stayed in our present community.

_____ The amount of job satisfaction I have now.

_____ The amount of job satisfaction I believe I will receive.

_____ Other reasons that are not listed here.

9. If we decided to move because of a job transfer, I would hope: *(You may choose more than one answer.)*

❏ My teens would be excited about the move.

❏ My teens would eventually forgive me.

❏ My teens would keep in touch with their friends.

❏ I have no expectations about how my teens would react to our moving.

10. If we decided to move because of a job transfer, I hope I: *(You may choose more than one answer.)*

❏ Would take time to be together with my spouse and teens.

❏ Would be successful so my family would be proud of me.

❏ Would be making the right move for the right reasons.

❏ Would be leaving for something, rather than running away from something.

11. If I could orchestrate the perfect move for my family, it would be:

12. God places us into various vocations during our lifetime (i.e., husband, wife, parent, student, employee, supervisor, neighbor, etc.). The Lord equipped me to be of service to others in these roles:

13. The strength I draw from Genesis 12:1 is:

147

Paul went to see them, and because he was a tentmaker as they were, he stayed and worked with them. (Acts 18:2b–3)

We've Been Downsized

It doesn't take long for teens to realize one of the greatest concerns of family life is money. There never seems to be enough; in fact, most families in today's society live paycheck to paycheck. It also doesn't take long for teens to develop the same fears their parents have, even if the parents haven't vocalized them. But what are parents to do, realizing we work for companies that might be prosperous one minute yet undergo a complete change in management the next, meaning we might be out of a job at any time? How can parents continue to reassure teenagers who share our fears that perhaps there won't be enough money?

At the heart of the unemployment crisis rests the age-old theological question: Will God remain faithful to His promise and continue to provide for our needs as a family? In Scripture, we can see God always provided for His people's needs. The apostle Paul is an example. God called Paul on the Damascus road and chose him to be an ambassador for Christ. As Paul responded to that call, he continued his profession as a maker of tents, trusting in God's ability to provide. Paul wrote in his letter to the Philippians, "I have learned the secret of being content in any and every situation, whether well fed, or hungry, whether living in plenty or in want. I can do everything through Him who gives me strength" (Philippians 4:12–13).

As parents, we can continue to trust that no matter what happens to our job situation, God will continue to provide for us and our families, giving us the strength to be content no matter what situation we might face.

What are we going to do now?

My name is Joanne. Ten years ago my husband Steve was killed in an auto accident, and I've been alone since. For the last five years I had a great job as a secretary to the CEO of a company. Now my company has been sold. A new CEO has been named and he wants his own secretary, so I'm out of a job. They gave me a great severance package, so I know we can survive for some time. But I'm worried about my kids, especially Alyssa. I'll let her tell you her side of the story.

My name is Alyssa. I've lived with my mom and two younger brothers in the same house since my dad died. My mom had a great job as an executive secretary. Now that the company has been sold, she's out of a job. She's been given some money, but I'm scared!

Mom says God will provide for us, but I'm not so sure. God doesn't have a car payment and a house payment. God doesn't buy clothes for my brothers and me. God doesn't put food on our table. My mom does all that; or at least, she did until now.

What would you do?

- Imagine you are Joanne's best friend, and Alyssa came to you expressing her fears. How would you respond?

- If Joanne came to you and asked what she should do about Alyssa. What would you say to her?

- List the problems Joanne faces. Of those problems, choose the one you think is the most difficult. How would you go about solving the problem?

- During this time of Joanne's unemployment, what do you believe is her greatest need?

- During this time of Joanne's unemployment, what do you believe is Alyssa's greatest need?

- What other information do you need to help you respond to this situation more effectively?

- React specifically to Alyssa's comment, "God doesn't have a car payment and a house payment." How would you respond?

If the time ever comes when we are without work, we need to recognize and deal with the fear and anxiety our teenagers may experience. We need to give them permission to express their fears and voice their concerns. By letting them do that, we affirm the validity of their thoughts and feelings. If that is the least we do as we begin the search for another job, we have done a great deal.

In the midst of the job search, however, we also need to be careful to let our teens know our employment situation is our problem, and in many respects, not theirs. We can let them know how much we appreciate their concern and worry; however, we need to let them see our resolve to solve our vocational crisis, as well as a possible financial crisis, on our own. If indeed we run into difficulty on both scores, we can assure our teens we will seek professional help to aid us in our job search, and help us sort through any emotional upheaval we might experience because of our job loss.

Behind our psychological, sociological, and economic concerns stands a God who provides for His creation and cares for us, His creatures. Throughout the periods of unemployment in our lives, we can depend upon the Lord to continue to provide and care for us. God can use periods of unemployment as a time to draw our families closer to Him. We can make worship a priority, staying rooted in Scripture and drawing strength from the meal at His Table. We can also use the time to evaluate the difference between our wants and needs; and perhaps think about the possibility of doing our own personal downsizing. As we survey our possessions, our finances, our wants, and our needs, perhaps we will be able to see more clearly what we really need in our lives, and how God in His infinite mercy is able to provide for those needs.

Finally, we need to remember we have been called to serve. Employed or not, we can trust that God will continue to give us the strength, the ability, and the willingness to be His servants, until we are with Him at last in heaven.

Closing Prayer

O God, You have called me to serve You, and You have given me talents and abilities to perform that service. Even when I find myself unemployed, continue to give me the strength to serve You as Your faithful child and as the faithful parent of the child You have given to me. In Your Son's name. Amen.

Parent Pairs

What would you say to your children if you worked for a company that down-sized you out of your position? What would be your greatest fear about losing your employment? What do you believe your child's greatest fear would be? What plans have you made, if any, in the event your company eliminates your position? What would you need from your church? What would you need from God?

Read Acts 18:2b–3 and consider the following questions as you discuss the **Parent Pairs** section with your spouse or another parent.

We've Been Downsized

(To be done with your spouse or another parent)

1. People who have been laid off because of downsizing need to continue to live out their lives in a normal fashion, no matter what the cost.

    Agree   Disagree

2. If I were laid off from work, I would be open and honest with my teens about my feelings and fears.

    Agree   Disagree

3. My greatest fear about being unemployed is: *(You may choose more than one answer.)*

    ❏ What my friends would say.

    ❏ That my self-esteem would suffer greatly.

    ❏ My ability to pay all my creditors.

    ❏ Having to go on unemployment compensation.

    ❏ Having to change my lifestyle.

    ❏ Other.

4. My teens' greatest fear about my unemployment is: *(You may choose more than one answer.)*

    ❏ What their friends would say.

    ❏ My emotional stability.

    ❏ Not having enough money to do what they want to do.

    ❏ Having to change their lifestyle.

    ❏ Possibly having to find a job.

    ❏ Other.

5. I have a plan that would work for my family if I were unemployed tomorrow.

Agree   Disagree

6. I have talked about the possibility of unemployment with my teens.

Agree   Disagree

7. I have been unemployed in the last five years.

Agree   Disagree

8. What helped my family and me get through my period of unemployment was:

9. If I were unemployed, the one thing I would say to my teens would be:

10. What would you need if you found yourself unemployed tomorrow?
    a. I would need to give up the following things:

    b. I would expect my teens to:

    c. I would hope my friends would:

    d. I would want my spouse to:

    e. I would hope my church would:

    f. When it comes to my credit cards, I would:

g. As a parent, I would want to:

h. I would look to God to:

11. The strength I draw from Acts 18:2b–3 is:

So they are no longer two, but one.
Therefore what God has joined together,
let man not separate. (Matthew 19:6)

What Do I Call Him?

Divorce has become such a common occurrence in today's society we can no longer say a typical family has both the biological mother and father living under the same roof. As divorce has continued to be a phenomenon, an increase to the nuclear family has occurred as well. Instead of one mother, there often is a mother and a stepmother; instead of one father, there often is a father and a stepfather. In some families, relationships become even more complicated.

For teenagers, the divorce of their parents is often the beginning of a lifelong grieving process as they recognize something is missing from their lives that they either never had, or never will have again. Teens who are grieving a divorce react in similar ways to those who grieve the death of a loved one. The same feelings are present; anger, the desire to replace the loved one, denial, bargaining, and depression are all common for children of divorced parents. It's no wonder then that teens of divorced parents often resist the idea of their parents getting married to other people. Their parents' remarriage can short-circuit their grieving process, to say nothing of destroying the hope that their parents will get back together.

God's intent that one man and one woman be married to each other for a lifetime seems to be discarded by at least half the couples who get married today. Despite this statistic and despite sin, hard hearts, and hurt that swirl around this painful reality, God cares about His people. He loves His people, and His grace extends full forgiveness and a new beginning in Christ even to those who find themselves in the throes of divorce. God also loves the children of divorce and continues to be with them to comfort them in the midst of their grief and provide healing for the wounds caused by divorce.

As parents and children experience the fragility of their relationships with one another, we need not be afraid to speak boldly about the relationship God has given us in His Son Jesus Christ. We need to remind and encourage one another that God's relationship to us will never be broken, and God will remain with us always, even unto the close of the age.

He's not my dad!

I'm Matt. I'm 15, and I've lived with my mom alone now for the past five years. She and my dad were divorced 10 years ago. Although they've been divorced that long, they've stayed good friends. Neither of them has married again. I see my dad every week and stay with him every other weekend.

The trouble is, my mom is now going to marry a man I can't stand. I mean, I can't stand the sight of him. He wants me to call him "dad." He thinks he can be really close to me, and do things with me like I was his son. Just because he doesn't have any kids, he thinks he can turn me into one of his own.

I wish my mom and dad were still together. I'm not sure I ever want to get married, especially if it's going to turn out like this.

What would you do?

- If you were a friend of the family and Matt came to you with his concerns, what advice would you give him?

- If you were a good friend of Matt's prospective stepfather, what advice would you give him?

- What is Matt's greatest fear in this situation?

- How could you help Matt deal with that fear?

- What do Matt's mom and dad need to do to help Matt adjust to the marriage and his concern that his new stepdad is trying to turn him into one of his own kids?

- If you were Matt's mother and Matt came to you and said he wished you and your ex-husband were still together so he could have a family, how would you respond?

The effects of divorce can be unsettling for teenagers, which means the challenges for parents are many. Amidst all other issues that need to be addressed, divorcing parents need to reassure their teens the divorce was not their fault. Far too often, teenagers live with the delusion that if they would have been more obedient or less argumentative, the stress of the marriage would not have been as great and a divorce would never have occurred. As divorcing parents absolve their teens from any blame, they also need to reassure their teens of the continuity of their love for them. The ability of each parent to communicate their continuing love for their teens, despite the end of their love for each other, will go a long way to guarantee the emotional security of their teenagers.

Divorce is a relationship failure that has an impact on everyone involved. As parents and teens struggle with the myriad issues of divorce, and especially as they work through present and future relationships, it is important to remember God's relationship with His people does not fail. He is faithful to His people even when we are not faithful to Him or to one another. However, God understands the meaning and pain of broken relationships. After all, it was humankind who broke their relationship with God, and it was God who suffered the pain for reconciling that relationship through the suffering and death of His only Son, Jesus Christ our Lord. As parents and teens of divorce experience the pain of a broken marriage, may they regularly seek solace through the Word and Sacrament and find peace in the knowledge that, through Christ, God's relationship with them will never end.

Closing Prayer

O God, as parents face the end of their relationship with each other, fill them with the peace that comes from our reconciled relationship with You. Provide parents with patience and kindness so their teenagers may know their relationship with them and You will continue. In Your Son's name. Amen.

Parent Pairs

How would you tell your children you were going to divorce your spouse? What would be your concerns? What would be your fears? If you had a friend going through a divorce, how could you help him or her? If you were divorced, what would your prayer be for yourself or for your children?

Read Matthew 19:6 and consider the following questions as you discuss the **Parent Pairs** section with your spouse or another parent.

What Do I Call Him?

(To be done with your spouse or another parent.)

1. If I were to divorce my spouse, I would want shared or joint custody of my children.

   Agree   Disagree

2. I really don't have to worry about how my teens would react in the case of divorce. After all, teenagers are stronger than anyone gives them credit.

   Agree   Disagree

3. I believe it is perfectly all right to use "Mom and Dad's staying together would be harmful for the children" as one of the reasons for divorce.

   Agree   Disagree

4. If I divorce my spouse, my main concern would be: *(Rank these in order of importance, with 1 being the most important and 10 being the least important.)*

   _____ That my spouse is fair in his or her treatment of me, and what is said to our children.

   _____ That my children be assured of the consistency of my love.

   _____ That my children know they are not to blame for the divorce.

   _____ That I treat my spouse fairly, and I do not speak against my spouse to my children.

   _____ That I am consistent in my financial support of our children.

   _____ That I wait at least a year to be involved in another relationship to give my children time to get used to the idea.

   _____ That I am able to show to my children I am able to get on with my life without my spouse, and do not spend an overt amount of time mourning my loss.

   _____ That I make each time I see my children quality time.

   _____ That I am able to support my spouse in his or her attempts to continue to be the parent of our children.

   _____ That my spouse is able to take care of our children in a way that does-not threaten them, or do emotional or spiritual damage to them.

5. If I ever were to divorce my spouse, three things I would say to our children are:

6. If my spouse were ever to divorce me, three main things I want said to our children are:

7. I would want my children's stepparent: *(You may choose more than one answer.)*

   ❑ To support my ex-spouse in the disciplining of our children.

   ❑ To be a friend first to my children, then a parent.

   ❑ To continue to reinforce the fact that I am their parent.

   ❑ To provide my children love and nurture in the same way that I would.

8. If I had a stepchild, I would want: *(You may choose more than one answer.)*

   ❑ To support my ex-spouse in the disciplining of our children and stepchildren.

   ❑ To be a friend first to my stepchildren, then a parent.

   ❑ To continue to reinforce the fact that I am not their real parent.

   ❑ To provide my stepchildren love and nurture in the same way their parents would.

9. If I were to divorce my spouse, my prayer for my spouse and for me would be:

10. If I were to divorce my spouse, my prayer for my children would be:

11. The strength I draw from Matthew 19:6 is:

We were therefore buried with Him through baptism into death in order that, just as Christ was raised from the dead through the glory of the Father, we too may live a new life. If we have been united with Him like this in His death, we will certainly also be united with Him in His resurrection. (Romans 6:4–5)

Even in Death

The suddenness with which death often appears; the unfinished business it leaves in its wake; the feelings of sorrow, guilt, sadness, anger, and remorse, can sweep through teens and their family members like never-ending tidal waves. The experience is made more difficult for teens because they have only just begun to recognize that they and the ones they love are mortal creatures. Death makes parenting difficult because we parents have to deal with our own grief while helping our teens deal with theirs. We not only grieve for one we've lost, we grieve for our teens as they grieve. When we lose a parent, we grieve that our teens have lost a grandparent; when they lose a friend, we feel their hurt and their pain as well as our own from knowing their lives will never be the same again.

Since cycles of grief are so unsettling to all who are involved, we parents need to be reassured that God gave His Son, Jesus Christ, to suffer, die, and rise again to defeat death for us. Our Baptism joins us to the suffering, death, and resurrection of our Lord and Savior; as we are baptized into Christ, we die with Him. The confidence of our baptized life rests in the assurance that since we have died already, death ultimately has no power over us. As parents, we need to share this reassurance with our teens. It gives us confidence, whether we face death ourselves or continue to live even within our grief, for St. Paul reassures us that nothing in all of creation will be able to separate us from the power of God's love in Christ Jesus our Lord (Romans 8:39).

Ultimately then, the way we approach death affects the way we choose to live. If death is the final word from God, we live out our lives in fear of death and thus become afraid to live. Yet if death is an experience that has been overcome by God through Jesus Christ, we can live our lives in faith, trusting death is not the final answer from God, and knowing our lives, safe with God, will never end. This knowledge and faith will to help us as we deal not only with our teenagers' grief, but also with our own.

I can't believe she's gone!

My name is Sheila and I want to tell you about my best friend, Tina. I can't believe she's gone. You see, she and I have known each other forever. Our moms were best friends. We were born a day apart in the same hospital in a rural Wisconsin town. In fact, we spent most of our first year together because our moms were such good friends.

Last Friday, on her way home from school, Tina was killed by a hit-and-run driver as she was crossing the street. I'm so angry. I have so many questions. I don't know why God allowed something terrible like this to happen to Tina. I don't know why someone would hit her and then just leave her there to die. I wonder if it's true what my pastor said in my religion class—is Tina in heaven? What is death like?

Today is her visitation, and I don't know if I want to go to the funeral home or the funeral. I'm so scared. I'd rather remember Tina the way she was while she was alive. I wish I knew what to do.

What would you do?

- If you were Sheila's parent, what would you say to her to address her fears?

- Say Sheila decides to ask you the questions about heaven and what death is like. How would you respond?

- Sheila is not sure she wants to go to the funeral home, since she would rather remember Tina the way she was when she was alive. As Sheila's parent, say why you would agree or disagree with her.

If you disagree, how would you help Sheila see it was important for her to attend the funeral, and perhaps go to the funeral home?

• Sensing Sheila's anger, confusion, fear, and sadness, and assuming you were experiencing some feelings as well, what would you share with her about your feelings for Tina?

• As Sheila's parent, how would you use Tina's death to teach her what you believe about death?

• As Sheila's parent, what would be the most helpful thing you could do for her as she experienced the loss of her friend?

• As a parent, how might you help Sheila understand that God understands her loss, and comforts her in her grief?

Grief has been defined as an emotional, spiritual, and physical reaction to a loss. In other words, when death comes, we are affected at every level. As we parents deal with our teenagers' grief as well as our own, we need to recognize grief can never be fixed quickly. In fact, some grief counselors have said it takes as many as five years before a person has grieved sufficiently to move on. As parents, we need to know any attempts to short-circuit that grief or speed up the process can cause our children unresolved problems later in life.

Our first task then, is to allow our children to feel, and validate any and every feeling they experience. Whether the feelings include anger at God, anger at themselves, or deep guilt because of unfinished business in the relationship, their feelings are valid simply because they feel them—even if we feel they are unwarranted.

Second, we need to be willing to be with our children as they experience their grief, meaning we remain with them although we may be experiencing our own grief. Grieving is perhaps the most difficult work we can do as parents and as humans. Grieving alone makes that work even more difficult. Our teens need to know we are there to support them in their hour of need and confusion.

Finally, if necessary, we need to reeducate our teens on the primary functions of a funeral: to help us say good-bye and to provide comfort in our sorrow as Christ is presented as Victor over sin and even our own death. These two functions operate together since the word "good-bye," as discussed in chapter 11, does teach us about the church's belief about death since it means *God be with you.*

Through the affirmation of our baptismal faith, we trust the God who remains with the friend or loved one who has died in the faith, remains with us now, and will remain with us until we say our final good-bye to our friends and loved ones here on earth. This faith helps us know that since we were buried with Christ by Baptism into His death, we already have died; and as a result, death has no power over us. May that affirmation of our hope comfort and strengthen us as we help our teens face the painful experience of the loss of friends or loved ones.

Closing Prayer

Loving God, You have promised us that nothing, not even death, will ever separate us from the power of Your love. Continue to be faithful to Your promise, O God, as I help my teens deal with their grief and point them to You, who overcame death for all who believe. In Jesus' name. Amen.

Parent Pairs

What are your thoughts about your own death? Have you discussed the eventuality of your death with your teens? When death strikes, what help can you give your teens to allow them to grieve? What help do you need from your church? How do you believe God can help you and your teens in times of grief and loss? What might your prayer be for your teens as they experience the loss of a friend or a loved one?

Read Romans 6:4–5 and consider the following questions as you discuss the **Parent Pairs** section with your spouse or another parent.

Even in Death

(To be done with your spouse or another parent.)

1. My teens have never lost a friend or a loved one.

   Agree   Disagree

2. My teens have been to a funeral.

   Agree   Disagree

3. The most important aspect of a funeral for me is: *(Rank these in order of importance, with 1 being the most important and 10 being the least important.)*

   ____ It allows me to see friends and relatives I haven't seen in a long time.

   ____ It gives me a chance to view my friend or loved one one more time.

   ____ It allows me to say good-bye to my friend or loved one.

   ____ It helps me remember that one day I too will die.

   ____ It gives me a chance to celebrate the faith I have in Jesus who triumphed over death.

   ____ It gets me a day off of work.

   ____ It helps me think about any unfinished business I might have with the people I love.

   ____ It helps me realize my days are numbered and makes me appreciate each day as a gift from God.

   ____ It allows me to be a teacher to my children.

   ____ It gives me an opportunity to support others who are in grief.

4. The three most important aspects of a funeral and why they are important are:

5. When my teens experienced the loss of a friend or a loved one, the three most helpful things I did for them were:

6. When my teens experienced the loss of a friend or a loved one, the three most harmful things I did for them were:

7. If I died while my teens were still adolescents, I would hope they would learn these three important things about my death:

8. When I die, I hope this epitaph would appear on my tombstone:

9. When I die, I really don't care how my loved ones dispose of my remains; I won't be alive to worry about it anyway.

Agree   Disagree

10. I believe God can help my teens grieve by:

11. My prayer for my teens as they face the loss of a friend or a loved one would be:

12. My church could best help me help my teens deal with the loss of a friend or loved one by:

13. The strength I draw from Romans 6:4–5 is:

Peace I leave with you; My peace I give you.
I do not give to you as the world gives.
Do not let your hearts be troubled
and do not be afraid. (John 14:27)

The Schoolyard Jungle

Nothing seems more frightening, especially during these past years, than sending our teens to school right after we hear about another school shooting. There was a time when parents could send their teens to school and know that at the end of the day, they would come home to their families safe and sound. The only violent encounter would perhaps have been some pushing and shoving during physical education or verbal intimidation during lunch.

Now the world of parents and teens has been turned upside down. Teens exist in a world that can be very cruel. Stereotypes and cliques rule social structures. Teens struggling with low self-esteem criticize and cut down others in a vain attempt to elevate their own status. The ready availability of firearms, the rage contained within the hearts and the minds of some teens, the vanquished feelings reflecting lack of hope, and a senselessness of purpose all contribute to the possibility that teens may decide to act out their rage and turn it against their classmates, teachers, and themselves. Given the climate of the times, it seems like eruptions in schools will continue, and our fears for our teens' safety will also continue to be very real.

In light of those concerns, we can remember that Jesus came into a world dominated by violence. The *Pax Romana*—Roman Peace—of Jesus' world was not established without price. After Jesus ascended into heaven, the violence against Christians—especially by the Roman empire—would be a part and parcel of the early church's existence. Perhaps that is why Jesus' words in John were so important. Jesus needed to remind the disciples that despite any violence they might experience, God had given them peace through the saving work He would accomplish on the cross. That peace was present in His presence—Christ Himself among them. That peace would have the power to transcend any violence that might occur in the disciples' lives and give them comfort and hope for the future.

As we struggle with our fears about the violent world in which we and our teens live, God continues to give peace even when the world cannot. Our peace is present in His body and blood, received at His Table. God speaks the promise of peace through His Word and gives us hope and courage to face our world and our teens' world with confidence, knowing He will embrace us with the power of His grace.

I don't want to go!

The following conversation took place between Gina, a sophomore at Kennedy High School, her mom, Stephanie, and her dad, Jack, the day students in Gina's high school were sent home early because of a bomb threat. It begins as Gina is getting ready to go to bed for the evening.

GINA: Mom, Dad, I don't want to go to school tomorrow.

STEPHANIE: Gina, somebody just phoned in a threat. They wanted to get out of school early today, that's all.

GINA: It's not a joke. I was in a chat room tonight with my friends on the net, and Jason said he read these kids' Web site, and they're serious. Today was just a practice run, tomorrow will be the real thing.

JACK: Gina, I don't think so. It couldn't happen here ...

GINA: Dad, you don't get it. It wasn't supposed to happen at all those other places either.

STEPHANIE: I don't know Gina. Your dad and I have to talk more about this.

GINA: Well I hope you do. You'd feel awful if it were true.

JACK: Try to get some sleep Gina. We'll let you know in the morning.

GINA: Please Mom and Dad. I'm really scared. ...

What would you do?

- Finish the conversation between Jack and Stephanie after Gina has retired for the evening.

- As Gina's parents, what other information might you want before you make a decision about Gina's attending school in the morning?

- What's missing here is any knowledge of what the administrators of Kennedy High School know, and what they're prepared to do to keep their students safe. If you were Gina's parents, what assurances would you want from the school administrators to help allay Gina's fears?

- If you were Gina, what would you have wanted from Jack and Stephanie to help you deal with your fears?

- How might Jack and Stephanie have been better listeners as they talked with Gina? If they were better listeners, what might they have asked Gina to help her with her fears?

- You have been given some information about a website that allegedly has been developed by fellow students of Gina. What would you do with that information?

As our teens are confronted with the potential of school violence, we need to realize their fears are very real. If their fears are real, then certainly, our fears are very real as well. Perhaps the place to begin our dialogue with our teens is to be open and honest about our fears. The more we are open with our teens about our fears, the greater the likelihood they will be open with their fears as well.

Teens need to know that we will take the time to listen to them. The more we create opportunities for our teens to talk with us—shutting off the stereo in the car, sitting down together for meals—the more they will trust us, especially during times when they feel stressed out or afraid. The more we talk with our teens, the more we will know when and why they feel safe, persecuted, misunderstood, enraged. By listening to them in as nonjudgmental a way as possible, they can depend on knowing we will be there for them and will help them sort out the myriad feelings they encounter as they navigate the schoolyard jungle.

Finally, as we are all guided by the God who gives us the peace that passes all understanding, perhaps the Serenity Prayer, written by Reinhold Niebuhr, can help both us and our teens as we deal with the world of violence in which we exist. We can be assured that God will give us the serenity, courage, and wisdom to deal with the violent world that surrounds and threatens us every day.

Closing Prayer

Loving God, grant me the serenity to accept the things I cannot change, the courage to change the things I can, and the wisdom to know the difference. Help me use that serenity and courage to bring Your peace to those who might be intent on violence. In Jesus' name. Amen.

Parent Pairs

Do you talk with your teens on a regular basis? What are your teens' greatest fears? Do your teens feel safe in their school? If they don't, what do they need to do about that fear? How can you respond to that fear? What can your teens do to feel safer in their school and your neighborhood? What can you do to make your schools and neighborhood safer? What is your prayer for your teens as they attend school? What is your prayer for the teachers or the administrators?

Read John 14:27 and discuss the following questions in the **Parent Pairs** section with your spouse or another parent.

The Schoolyard Jungle

(To be done with your spouse or another parent.)

1. On average, I talk with my teens ____ .

    a. Ten minutes a day

    b. Twenty minutes a day

    c. An hour a day

    d. Every day

    e. Twice a week

    f. Once a week

    g. Once a month

    h. Never

    i. So many times, I can't keep track of the number.

2. If I could change one thing about how often I talk to my teens, it would be:

3. My teens usually come to me when they are worried or afraid.

    Agree   Disagree

4. I believe my teens' school is relatively safe and free from violence.

    Agree   Disagree

5. I believe our neighborhood is relatively safe and free from violence.

    Agree   Disagree

6. My teens believe their school is relatively safe and free from violence.

    Agree   Disagree

7. My teens believe our neighborhood is relatively safe and free from violence.

    Agree   Disagree

8. If there were two things I could do to make our neighborhood relatively safe and free from violence, I would:

9. If there were two things I could do to make my teens' school relatively safe and free from violence, I would:

10. I believe my teens' three greatest fears are:

11. Knowing my teens' fears and my fears about school violence, I need from my school administration:

12. Knowing my teens' fears and my fears about school violence, I need from my church:

13. As I think about school violence, my prayer for the teachers and administrators of my teens' school is:

14. As I think about school violence, my prayer for my teens is:

15. The strength I draw from John 14:27 is: